Like Father

LIKE FATHER

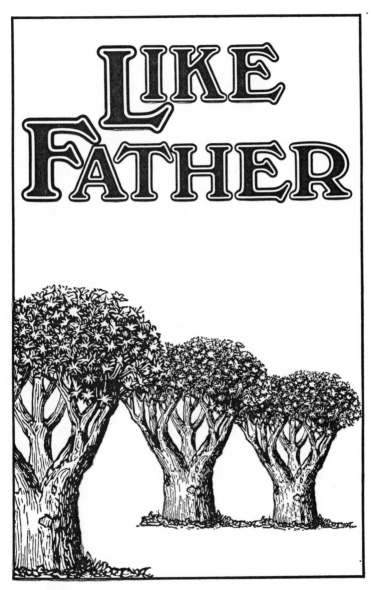

by **David Black**

Red Dembner Enterprises Corp. / New York

Dembner Books
Published by Red Dembner Enterprises Corp.
Distributed by Dodd, Mead & Company, New York
Copyright © 1978 by David Black
Printed in the United States of America

Design by Judith Michael

Portions of this book originally appeared in The Atlantic,
Harper's Magazine, Pequod, and Transatlantic Review.

Library of Congress Cataloging in Publication Data
Black, David
Like Father
I. Title
PZ4.B62694Li   [PS3552.L32]   813'.5'   78-6841
ISBN 0-396-07587-8

For Deborah and Susannah

Like Father

One

When my father was fifty-eight years old, after reading Henri Troyat's biography of Tolstoy, he ran away from home. Having packed a red wool shirt, a faded pair of Levi's, a change of underwear, and three pairs of gray ski socks, he walked the mile from his house on Maplewood Terrace to Route 91 North and, sticking out his thumb, hitched a ride with a Friendly Ice Cream Shop manager to West Springfield, where after a wait of half an hour he picked up a second ride with a teenaged boy traveling from Staten Island to Warwick, Massachusetts, to visit a religious commune called the Brotherhood of the Spirit.

"They sleep during the day," my father later explained to us, his eyes squinting in the dim light of the single sixty-watt bulb that swung above our kitchen table through clouds of insects, "and farm at night. Their leader is twenty-two years old, twenty-two, twenty-three, Michael somebody, a Greek name, and he also sings in a rock band. These communities interest me. . . ."

A third ride with a dairy farmer along Route 116 to

Route 47 brought my father within seven miles of the farmhouse that Maxie and I had rented.

"I asked the farmer about these communes," my father said. "He seemed to like them. He kept saying over and over that his two sons couldn't wait to go to New York or San Francisco and that he admired the kids who left the cities to farm. It made me proud of you. . . ."

Before leaving Springfield, my father had written a letter which he gave to me with a warning not to read until after he'd gone. His destination was unclear. Nova Scotia perhaps, Wyoming, Mexico. The letter said:

Dear Dennis, when you were seven under an influence we were never able to determine—Hopalong Cassidy, Tom Corbett and His Space Cadets, probably one of your television heroes—you ran away from home.

We found you around the corner, pushing along on your scooter. Since you hadn't left in anger, you evidently thought when you saw us that we'd come to give you a cheerful send-off.

You were enraged when we demanded that you turn your scooter around. We were being unreasonable in aborting your adventure.

I have no doubt that I will be as unsuccessful now as you were then. The terribly embarrassing thing is not being able to explain why one left in the first place.

I left your mother an inadequate note. Undoubtedly she'll also see this one, which won't explain anything either.

I didn't leave because I was unhappy. I wasn't angry. I wasn't suffocating. But I am running away. From what? Nothing.

I may not be able to tell you these things—not that any of them are particularly revealing—when I see you, but I did want to leave you with some kind of comment. At least an intimate gesture.

When we meet, both of us I'm sure will be too disturbed (or embarrassed) to make any kind of peace with each other.

For twenty-eight years, my father had taught English in the Springfield public school system with the passionate conviction that he was saving souls, although, because he was an atheist, he never would have phrased it that way. He had been raised in the Mount Sinai Orphanage in Boston as an orthodox Jew and had early abandoned Yahweh to the adults in the home who beat him when he misbehaved and ignored him when he didn't.

His father, my grandfather Aaron, deserted his children in 1921, freeing himself to scheme for various unattained fortunes. The few times he showed up at the orphanage to take my father on outings, after delicatessen lunches—whitefish with lemon, knockwurst and sauerkraut, lox, knishes, pirogi—he would give my father bootleg gin to deliver. My father's most horrible childhood experience, he once told me, was when he tripped climbing onto a trolley and smashed a bottle. Terror of police and shame at having failed overwhelmed him. He watched the trolley clatter away and then, sneaking through alleys and yards, raced to the orphanage, convinced that he would be sent to the reformatory.

His second most horrible childhood experience, he said, was when he was angry with his older brother, Abraham, for beating him up in the school yard. While Abraham was showering, my father threw a canful of lye at him. Abraham, screaming, shot flat against the shower wall, his back and right side puffing like burning marshmallow. My father rushed into the orphanage kitchen, stole a half-pound slab of butter—for which he was later thrashed—and, crouching in the fetid, gray, dormitory shower, smeared the butter over his brother's quivering body.

Abraham goaded the orphanage kids to fight the Catholic gangs in the neighborhood. In a side street behind a kosher butcher shop, he was knifed in the chest. My father, although shorter and younger than the others, fought for and gained control of the Mount Sinai gang, to lead them in a war against those who had killed his brother, to prove he was tougher than his brother had been.

To reinforce his leadership, my father staged a raid on the food stores in the orphanage cellar, escaping punishment by hiding in a flour barrel when he heard one of the cooks coming down the stairs. He led his cronies to the fourth-floor laundry chute, down which he jumped, sixty feet. The expected billowing pile of sheets was not waiting for him below. My father shattered his leg, driving the bone two inches into his hip. Terrified of punishment, my father hobbled on his smashed limb for the rest of the day, twisted in a white pain through the night, and fainted at the washroom sink the following morning.

While in the hospital, he did chin-ups on a bar that he had placed across his bed and, once on his feet, learned to throw his crutch; so when, back on the street, he was taunted by gang members who stood just out of reach, he was able to turn the crutch into a successful weapon. After cracking one tormentor's spine and permanently paralyzing him, my father was sent into a special disciplinary ward, where he learned woodwork, printing, and how to play the trumpet.

One of his teachers, a wire manufacturer's twenty-six-year-old daughter who had insisted on working with the incorrigibles, having been attracted by my father's intelligence, spent hours with him after classes, giving him books, playing him scratchy 78's of Bix Beiderbecke. On a rainy afternoon, while listening to "Mississippi Mud" with Bing Crosby and Frank Trambauer on vocals, my father ran his hand up her skirt.

She slapped him. He slapped her back just as her boyfriend, a Harvard graduate student in mathematics, walked in the door. To escape what he assumed would be a stretch in the reformatory, my father left the orphanage that night. He was seventeen, a fair trumpet player with a love for jazz and a determination to go to college.

He got a job in New York at a club called the Blue Room, sitting in for the regular trumpet player, a man named D'Agostino, who was dead drunk when he wasn't gambling and gambling when he should have been performing at the club. One night in a poker game with D'Agostino and Larry Craft, a gangster with a bad stomach who drank alternately from a tumbler of rye and one of cream, my father exploited a remarkable luck. Whatever they played—Mad July, Pope's Nose, Five Card Stud (my father's favorite), or classic Five Card Draw—my father won on the cards. Or successfully bluffed. The few hands he lost were small pots. My father, an attentive card player who could accurately estimate odds, folded early when he did not have a winning hand. Craft seemed to trust magic more than strategy: he bet heavily on hands every time he felt his luck turning, and the more he lost, the more optimistic he became.

After two hours, my father had won more than a thousand dollars from Craft. My father knew that Craft would allow him to win a few hundred without causing trouble, but he figured it would be unhealthy for him to leave the game a thousand dollars ahead. For the next few hours, my father unsuccessfully tried to lose some of the money back to Craft, who, convinced that my father could not keep winning, kept raising: two high pair against my father's straights, straights against my father's flushes, flushes against my father's full-houses. By three in the morning, my father had won over three thousand dollars from Craft.

D'Agostino had dropped out of the game and was nervously watching. He liked my father and didn't want to see him hurt. My father offered to quit and give Craft his money back. Craft, an honorable man, said no, my father had won the money fairly; he wasn't going to accept it back as a favor. "Let's keep playing," he said grimly. My father dealt the cards.

At dawn, Craft was almost ten thousand dollars in the hole. My father had never played in a game in which more than three hundred dollars had passed hands. Exhausted, his head aching, his belly sour, my father wanted to lose the money and go home to bed. Whenever my father lost a hand, Craft, sure that my father had finally hit a downward skid, would suggest doubling the stakes; and my father, hoping Craft was right about how his luck was running out, would row.

Finally, my father offered to cut the cards for his entire winnings. Craft, also tired and tense, cut first: a jack. My father pulled a king. They cut again: Craft, a nine; my father, a jack. And again: Craft a six; my father a four. They stared at the cards.

"I won," Craft said.

My father left the table and went into the bathroom to throw up. He flushed the toilet and watched the water swirl the brown and yellow vomit down the bowl. He leaned his forehead against the cool rim of the toilet seat. When he returned to the room where they had been playing poker, Craft was gone.

"He said he envies you," D'Agostino told my father. "You're the luckiest player he ever met. You deserved the whole pot."

Craft had left my father three thousand dollars out of the forty-thousand-dollar marker my father would have taken home if they had quit before the last cut of the deck.

My father taxied home and, before going to bed, wrote a letter asking for an application for admission to Boston University. He conned and wheedled his way into the B.A. program. Between the money he'd saved and the money he'd won, he had enough to pay for tuition and living expenses for two years.

He did well, skidding from scholarship to scholarship for eleven years, during which time he collected a dozen languages, an uneasy but extensive acquaintance with English literature, a library of over two thousand books, three degrees, and a wife.

He met my mother while he was living in Gloucester, Massachusetts, with four other members of the Western Socialist Party, a pure Marxist conspiracy so innocent that they were not banned from agitating on Boston Common during World War II. The five of them had rented three cabins near the beach. My father lived alone. One Saturday, he cleaned house, threw the trash into the fireplace to burn, and, having left some records stacked on the mantel, walked down the road for a swim.

Ethel Diamond, the twenty-four-year-old social worker who within a year would become my mother, was visiting her sister and her new brother-in-law.

In a photograph taken of her that summer, she stands, her black bathing suit showing a ladder of horizontal creases up her belly, her hands hidden (perhaps clasped) behind her back, demure and sweet, sexy and chubby, not at all like the woman who raised me. At a family gathering many years later, my aunt accused my mother of marrying my father to compete with her. My aunt had just gotten married; my mother did not want to be left behind—the older sister—in youthful spinsterhood. My mother, blushing, claimed she didn't want to marry at all—or at least not so young. My father, a roughneck, had swept her into love against her will. She had only wanted a flirtation, but had been caught by the undertow of his personality.

That summer afternoon, she threw (accidentally? on purpose? she claims it was a mistake) a beach ball at my father, who was stalking out of the water. He tossed it back. They introduced themselves. He wooed her with an economy of words—and well-placed hands. She agreed to walk to his cabin for coffee and cake. On the path they met the postman, who said, "Do you live in the number two cabin up that way?"

My father said, "Yes."

"Well," said the postman, walking on and looking at the letters he was shuffling, "it's burning to the ground."

When I was a child and my father would sit, in the twilight, on the edge of my bed telling me the story, at this point I would bolt up with a knot in my chest, as though I had swallowed a hard ball of cold water, and say, "The records caught on fire, didn't they?"

He would nod and stand, making the mattress bounce, and say as he walked through the gloom to my bedroom door, "That's right. They were made of shellac and caught on fire from the trash in the fireplace."

And once, when I was older, almost too old to be told bedtime stories, I said, "That was pretty stupid, leaving them on the mantel, wasn't it?"

My father paused in the door, a dark shape against the hall dusk.

"Yes," he said, "it was stupid." And then, half in anger, half in puzzlement, he added, "Don't you know most of life is made up of stupid mistakes?"

I said, "It isn't."

"Good night," said my father.

"It isn't," I repeated; and, as I felt my hold on my father weakening—he was backing into the hall, making "Calm down" gestures with his hands—I screamed, "It isn't! It isn't! It isn't!"

My father stopped his retreat and reentered the bedroom.

"You're in a nice rage," he said.

"No, I'm not," I said, throwing myself back on the bed.

"That's all right," he said. "It's all right to be in a rage. If I hadn't been in a rage, I never would have gone to college. And I'm glad I went." He stood, staring down at me. I twisted like the grubs I used to impale in the backyard. "But save the rage for something worthwhile," he said at last, "because you can use it up on worthless things; and when you need it for something important, it's gone."

The evening my father arrived at our farmhouse, Maxie and I were in the garden. I was squatting by the pole beans, plucking the few left on the vine for our supper. Maxie was kneeling by a cucumber mound, searching for a cucumber that wasn't rotten or overripe.

She straightened and, stepping over the mound,

said, "Some old man just walked up our front porch."
She turned to me. "Dennis?"

I came down the path between the furrows. My father, still carrying his suitcase, had circled back into sight around the corner of the house. He strolled, glancing up at the second-floor porch, where a Mexican hammock hung. Abandoned books, our current fancies (*Vikram and the Vampire*, Hammett's *Red Harvest*, Father Brown, Lovecraft's map of local western Massachusetts horrors, what else, some books on education, some books on garden insects, a book of popular astronomy with which Maxie and I tried to decipher the night sky), made human-looking lumps—buttocks, shoulder, elbow—in the hammock's blue web. My father put down his suitcase and called up at the shape he assumed was a resting body.

"Hello," he shouted. "Dennis? Maxie?"

The books in the hammock did not resolve themselves into some head, arms, and torso; did not sit up and peer down at my father; did not answer.

"Hey," my father called, "wake up, Dennis. Greet your prodigal pop. I've suddenly become a dropout."

The sun was behind us, balanced on the horizon, large and round as a yawn. When I shouted to him, my father turned and put his hand to his forehead in a salute to shade his eyes.

Bluff and grinning—the bared teeth occasionally turning into a manic grimace—my father described his day's adventures.

"Running away was the climax," he said. "The rest will be an extended, increasingly painful denouement."

13 | *Like Father*

Later at dinner, his elbows propped up on the table, my father continued to sketch his running away as though it were a neatly, already completed play. His voice vibrated with the same wheedling urgency that balanced his lectures on a nice edge of curiosity. When I was a freshman in college, one vacation I sat in on his class, partly to judge him with the mean, keen eye of a nineteen-year-old son, partly to probe into the eager pride he roused in me.

He started the class by saying—I wrote it down, irked at having been nudged from my role as critical son into that of appreciative student—"By lumping certain of Shakespeare's plays together under the title of tragedies, you imaginatively annihilate the great differences among them. *Macbeth* touches our scorn as much as our pity. *Hamlet* moves us to an ecstasy of frustration. But it's impossible to read *Lear* without weeping."

That struck me as extraordinary: "It's impossible to read *Lear* without weeping."

I had just read it for a humanities course and hadn't wept. I was sure none of my father's students had wept. My friends at college dutifully had venerated it, but as far as I knew no one had wept. I was half sure my father hadn't wept when reading it, that his speech was mere showmanship.

But there was something in the certainty with which he said it—the absolute conviction that one could not really read the play, understand it, and believe in the old king's despair without shedding tears—that sprung some valve of respect.

At home, my father faltered from one decision to another: should he buy a new car, put up the screens, call so-and-so on the School Committee to protest the exclusion of *A Connecticut Yankee in King Arthur's Court* from the list of books to be bought for the following year, wear a white or a pale blue shirt to a retirement dinner . . . At home, when I would confront him with a bristling assertion that I knew contradicted his opinion ("Wolfe wasn't a very good writer, was he, Dad?"), he would clear his throat, hesitate, temporize, shrug.

In class, there he was, speaking *ex cathedra!* And he seemed to be right.

That evening and for weeks thereafter, I tried to elicit the same sureness from him—about books, music, politics, flavors of ice cream, anything. But he would squint his eyes in pain and, my insistence prickling up against him, step back, step back again, dropping *maybe*'s and *perhaps*'s along the path of his retreat, as though he were trying both to escape and to leave a trail for me to follow.

I couldn't follow him, however—at least, not into his blinking, shrugging insecurity; not even into smiling, cautious ambiguity. I wanted him to be certain, to be absolute, to slam his fist onto a tabletop and say, "Look, kid, you're wrong." But he refused to give me any further demonstration of what I assumed to be his rigid and correct self.

That night, trying to sound casual, but giddy at the prospect of rupturing the traditional membrane of polite ignorance of each other's intimate motives or excuses that separated us, I asked my father why he always had evaded my questions.

"Your questions?" my father murmured. "Your questions? Did you ever really want to know what I thought? I always felt you were throwing some kind of noose over my head, and if I resisted the rope would slip tighter."

"Did you think that?" I asked, apparently surprised, but feeling that he was right and that I had known it all along. "Did you really think I was trying to trap you?"

"Weren't you?" he asked, the pained furtive glance slipping into his eyes like sizzling drops of water skittering onto a hot skillet.

We both flinched, paused at the moment when only anger or love would have carried us into each other's sealed world. I tapped my knee with fingers that abruptly seemed large and clumsy. My father crossed his legs and thrust his hands deep into his pockets. His chin touched his chest; and, blinking up over the tops of his glasses, he exchanged one dangerous subject for another.

"Well," he said in an innocent treble, "when am I going to be a grandfather?"

"What do you want to be a grandfather for?" I said. "Isn't being a father hard enough?"

"Hard?" he asked.

"Are you in a hurry to be one?" Maxie leaned back stiffly in her chair, the same way she tenses herself when we're in the car and I take a curve too fast.

Unsure whether Maxie was joking or provoking

him, he said, "You've been married seven years. I was a father well before our first anniversary."

"Marvelous," said Maxie, "how did you manage that?"

"Should I explain the facts of life?" my father asked.

"I know all about them," said Maxie. "You find babies under cabbages. That's what we're growing in our garden. Dennis, why are you shaking your head at me?"

"Why are you being unpleasant?" I asked.

My father, trying to appease Maxie by defending her, accused me.

"You're always finding something wrong," he said. "She's just having a joke."

"I'm not *she*," said Maxie. "Call me by my name."

"What are you yelling at me for?" said my father. "I'm on your side."

"My side?" she said. "What are you talking about? I don't have a side."

Desperately attempting not to be misunderstood, terrified that my father would dismiss her anger as something that he, as a male, could charm away, she grabbed his hands and pulled him toward her.

The contact was not sexual, but an effort to make him know the hungry something in her that wielded her femininity like a weapon. My father became tensed attention, sensing the merely erotic.

"I want a baby," she said.

"Then why don't you have one?" my father asked.

"Because I'm not ready," I said.

The emotional acceleration stopped. There was a

noticeable lag in our responses. None of us was sure what had happened. My father untangled his hands from Maxie's grasp and folded them on the table.

"Dennis has this thing about fatherhood," said Maxie, her voice flat, although her neutral tone had set up a flag: this is where I can be hurt; don't hurt me. "Dennis thinks that fathers have to choose between destroying their children or being destroyed by them."

"What about us?" my father asked me. "Do you think I destroyed you?"

Suddenly exposed by his assumption—"Do you think *I* destroyed *you?*"—he started shaking his head no, as though to cue me; and in doing so he typically was offering himself for the sacrifice. He was saying: given the choice between your destruction or my destruction, let us agree upon doing me in.

"Well," he said, "do you think you destroyed me?"

The question was rhetorical. Neither of us was prepared to admit the answer. My father quickly said, "We were talking about babies." But it sounded as though he had said: let's talk about something less important than this male struggle of ours; let's talk about some trifling woman's complaint. "We were talking about babies."

Maxie spilled her coffee over the table. My father grabbed a napkin and began mopping up the mess. When he finished, he stuffed the dripping napkin into a glass.

"It's bedtime," he said. "I'm tired." At the bottom of the stairs, he half turned. "Ah, Dennis, I haven't quite settled where I'm going yet. Would it be too much of an inconvenience if I stayed here for a day or two?"

I said, "No. I'd like that."

"Good." He started to go.

"Stay as long as you want."

"Good," he repeated.

"This is as good a place to run away to as any other," I said, realizing as I spoke that willfully, although unconsciously, I had maimed him as surely as if I had laid a hot poker across his face.

He made a noise halfway between a snort and a guffaw and, having said a gloomy good night, climbed the stairs to his bedroom.

"Are you afraid your son will hate you as much as you hate him?" Maxie asked. She was testing me: if I could hate him, couldn't I also hate her?

"I don't want to have to be a model," I said.

"Do you think we could have a baby in a year?" she said, invoking one of our catechisms. We had fixed scripts for exorcising all the devils of anxiety, anger, love, lust, all the insistent affects that threatened to crowd habit and security from our lives. By varying the old questions and answers slightly every time we walked through our roles, we safely sneaked forward toward being the people we wanted to become. When Maxie asked, "Do you think we could have a baby in a year?" she was saying: I'm frightened; I don't recognize you; play your role.

"Yes, in a year," I should say.

"Yes, in a year we should be settled enough . . ." I should say.

"Yes, in a year. Of course, it depends . . ." I should say.

As in a guessing game, you must try one variation

after another until you find the one that fits, the correct answer.

I said: "I don't want a baby."

"I don't believe you," said Maxie. "You're lying. Aren't you? Aren't you?" Her need had claws. I had not been lying. I had been exploring a growing panic. In bed, when she put her hands flat against my back and asked again, "Weren't you lying?" I gave her, instead of love, the devious gift of a soothing answer: "I was lying, yes."

Maxie and I slept in a large room behind the kitchen to take advantage during cold weather of the fireplace, across from which we had placed our bed. Sometime before dawn, a noise woke me; and, peering into the dark kitchen, I found my father, luridly lit by the blue and yellow ring of flame on the gas stove.

He wore only his tan slacks, no shirt or shoes, and was whistling Kate Smith's theme song, "When the Moon Comes Over the Mountain." As he poured steaming water from a tea kettle over the coffee in the Melitta filter, he began singing in a low, nasal, Vaughn Monroe style. The piddling stream of dripping coffee accompanied him. After clanking the kettle back onto the stove and turning off the gas, he switched to a Bing Crosby version of "Because My Baby Don't Mean Maybe Now."

It was too dark to see him, but I heard him shuffling in an easy soft-shoe to his own music. I gauged the distance between our worlds as the difference between Crosby's chorus, nonsense sounds that slid from his mouth like water dribbling through parted lips—"Buh buh ba la, buh buh ba la, ba la"—and the music I would have babbled in the dark, a fierce spray of sound, Little Richard Penniman's "A wop bop a loo mop a lam bam boom . . ."

Not that different after all, because somehow the relaxed syllables of my father's song and the angry syllables of mine both slipped a wedge between the singer and seriousness. Neither chorus meant anything. Or rather, both choruses meant something more than words could have expressed. They were magic chants to invoke some spook of youth. Standing in the dark and letting "Tutti Frutti" bop in my mind beside the music my father was making, I for the first time felt old.

Up until that moment, I still had thought of myself as, say, nineteen. Perhaps twenty or twenty-one at the most. I was stunned. I could slide my imagination back a decade and discover myself as essentially the same person who was standing in the dark kitchen, secretly listening to my father jolt through a repertoire of early jazz and swing. I had a history! I felt like a lucky archaeologist who stumbles onto a terrain fertile with artifacts of an unknown civilization: intact temples buried under soil pocked with pottery, weapons, primitive games, uncrushed skulls, tools, coins, bracelets . . .

The screen door creaked open and banged shut, and I saw a hole in the dark move across the lawn. I followed, also letting the screen door bang to alert my father to my presence.

"Maxie?" he asked. "Dennis?"

"Dennis," I said. "You're up early."

"I couldn't sleep," he said. "Sorry I disturbed you."

"I couldn't sleep either," I lied, trying to force an intimacy by admitting to a similar complaint. I couldn't say I was sorry for hurting him earlier, because by acknowledging the injury I would only enlarge it. To establish contact, I had to make myself vulnerable, but I couldn't think of anything sufficiently sensitive. Ever since we left New York and moved to the farm, my life had been remarkably uneventful, happy. The slight annoyances of the past year were not substantial enough to offer up as a token of my defenselessness. It was like finding myself at the altar of some bloodthirsty god with only a chipmunk to slaughter and a knife too frail for suicide.

So I lied again, sketching a general anxiety to explain my insomnia. My father rose to the bait, gave the lie flesh by making connections I had not implied.

"Are you having problems with Maxie?" he asked.

Since his question had a slight tremor of intimacy—the father probing the son's misery with the same delicacy used to tease out a splinter with a needle and the same possibility of having to dig painfully into the flesh—I assumed my father felt he'd found a sensitive spot.

"Yes," I said, "a little."

Ready to jab a nerve, he asked, "Is she unfaithful?"

We were exchanging hostages: I won't hurt you if you won't hurt me. I hoped we would make more exchanges, inching closer to each other with each revelation.

It would be painful to admit that Maxie was unfaithful (even though as far as I knew she wasn't), but I supposed my father would not make any deadly attacks.

And even if I were wrong and he did, my confidence was a fraud. I wasn't ready to trust my father that entirely. So once more I lied.

"Yes," I said.

He said, "I'm sorry."

"It's nothing serious," I said.

My father laughed—sympathetically, I thought.

"You don't sound convincing," he said, and after a pause added, "Well, she's a very attractive woman. Are you going to separate?"

"I don't know," I said.

"Look, Dennis," he said, "you can talk to me." Without stopping, however, to let me talk, he continued, "That would have some kind of neatness to it. Both of us leaving our wives at the same time. We could become hoboes together." There was another pause. When he laughed again, he had changed his position. I turned quickly around, chilled, as though I feared he would attack me if I let him get behind me.

"Do you want a drink?" I asked.

"What do you have?"

"Jack Daniel's?"

"OK," he said.

I walked back into the house to get the bottle. On my way out, I hesitated, tiptoed to my bedroom, and, feeling in the dark for Maxie's head, kissed her on the cheek. She murmured something and flung an arm up over my neck, pulling me down to kiss me on the side of my mouth. Feeling reassured—I didn't want my lie to conjure up some infidelity—I went outside into the chilly morning. The dark had become gray, and I could make out my father's face.

I offered him the bottle. He drank, wiped his lips with the back of his hand, and handed the liquor back. I drank, gave him the bottle, which he held at his side.

"That's some garden," he said. "That's some garden you've got back there."

"Yeah," I said, slowly moving in that direction beside him. "It's the thing that makes sense out of this place. We're very proud of it." My throat tightened. Here was a revelation, although I wasn't sure that my father would understand. "When we came here," I said, "I was very unsure about giving up a lot of things. Ambition. You know, trying to be a success. Making it in New York. It was like all that was the bone in my life. All winter I'd get these flashes of desperation. I felt completely abandoned. We left this place only a dozen times between October and March—except to drive into the Piggly-Wiggly for food. No one ever came out here. Too far.

"It got so I couldn't read a paper or watch TV without getting terrified and angry. Running scared. Things were happening. I thought they were important. We didn't even know about the Manson trial until months afterward. Funny. It was like being stuck in a dream and not being able to get out. Even though it was a fairly pleasant dream. I wanted to go back to New York. Maxie wanted to stay here."

"So that's where the trouble started," said my father.

Yes, I thought, there had been trouble between Maxie and me. Not what my father had assumed and I had pretended, but just as serious. Being vulnerable to another, it seemed, was also being vulnerable to yourself. And the real revelations surprise both of you.

"It wasn't true what I said before about Maxie," I said.

My father grunted. I wasn't sure he believed me.

"Not in the way I meant it, at least," I added. "But there was . . ."

"Was?"

"Is . . . a little, I guess . . . is a breach. I only said that other thing because—because it seemed like you wanted to believe it and—"

"Like I want to believe it?" my father interrupted. "Why would I want to believe Maxie was unfaithful?"

"I don't know," I said. "Why would you?"

It had gotten much lighter. We were standing on the edge of the garden. My father tipped back the bottle and took a long drink, after which he handed it to me. I drank, capped the bottle. My father said:

"I envy you, Dennis. I envy you your age, the times in which you grew up, your generation, the fact that you could escape New York, ambition, whatever, I envy you this." He waved to the garden. "Yeah," he said, "this."

We were walking around the garden. I said:

"In the spring, when we planted, all the terrors vanished. It was like watching things grow, having helped them grow, healed all the raw things inside."

"Yes," said my father, "and when winter comes?"

I sighed.

"That," I said, "terrifies me. It's like thinking about death."

"I think about death a lot," said my father. "I figure I've got a decade left. Ten years. Can you imagine that? Ten years." He made a noise that was the beginning of a laugh. "Next year it'll be nine years. Then eight. Then seven. Can you imagine that?"

"Yes," I said.

"No, you can't. No, you can't. What are you? Thirty. You're still invulnerable. Nothing can hurt you."

I started to say something, but he interrupted:

"Shut up. You don't know . . . You don't know . . ." He put a hand over his eyes. "Wouldn't that be remarkable? If I started to cry. God, I envy you. How were you able to do this? How?" He reached up and grabbed an overhanging branch with both hands. "Goddamn me," he said. "Goddamn me, but I want to do something outrageous."

My father went in to bed. I stayed up, made two soft-boiled eggs, which I ate while sitting in the porch rocker and listening to the birds, and an hour later left for Martin's Stables, where I worked three days a week in the barn, shoveling up manure that I spread in the fields to fertilize the grass that was cut, baled, and carted back into the barn for the horses to eat. Once I asked Mr. Martin why he didn't let the horses graze in the fields and in the natural course of events spread the manure themselves. Tipping his red bald head to the side and opening his eyes wide, he said:

"But, my friend, that wouldn't make sense, would it?"

The day was hot; the evening was warm. When I returned home at six-thirty, Maxie dropped her hoe and ran around the tomato plants toward me. She was pointing behind herself at the woods.

"I want him to leave," she said. "I want him to leave tonight." Her face was sunburned, and there was a dried spot of blood on her forehead where she had squashed a mosquito. "He tried to make love to me today. I was swimming in the stream. He'd followed me down. I guess, since I didn't have any clothes on, he took that as some sort of invitation . . ." She waved her hands in front of her face to brush away bugs. A drop of sweat slid from her right temple down her smudged cheek and trembled on her chin. She slapped at it. "Damn flies," she said.

"What did he do?" I asked.

"He touched me," she said.

"Where?" I asked.

"On the breast," she said. "Why? Does it matter?"

She was impatient with me, as though my question implied I saw her as a target, each part of her body worth a certain number of points. Her hand five points, her shoulder ten, her breasts fifty, her crotch one hundred.

"Would you feel different if he just touched my arm?" she asked. "I wouldn't."

"Where is he?" I asked, some Oedipal nerve lighting up like a pinball machine.

She gestured. I circled around the garden and climbed the hill into the woods. The path twisted through thick pines, some hickory, birch, beech, red and silver maple . . . After peeling a curl from a black birch, I put the bark under my tongue and let the taste of wintergreen fill my mouth. That and the smell of the purple milkweed blossoms that hung on the top of the knee-high stalks in sunny patches fixed the moment for me. There was an awful joy seeping through the locks in my brain. If I had found my father then, I would have killed him.

I walked for fifteen minutes until I came to the slope that led down to the stream. Floating in the shallow water, face up, eyes closed, his mouth warped into a miserable grin, my father looked very old. Stopping at the edge of the bank, I said, "Put your clothes on."

My father opened his eyes.

"I've been waiting for you," he said. "I stayed down here after Maxie left. I couldn't bear to be with her after what I did."

I said, "Get out of the water and get dressed."

"At first," he said, still not moving, just floating there, "I was terrified of what would happen when you got back. It was a curious feeling, to be terrified of one's son. I had all sorts of strange thoughts. If we fought, I figured you'd have the advantage; and I even felt bad that I hadn't beat the shit out of you when you were a kid. You know? To make up for whatever you might do to me today. Then I thought: what the hell, this is what we've both been waiting for. All that talk this morning. You didn't want to get close to me because you loved me. You wanted to get close enough to—"

"If I'm going to beat the shit out of you," I said, "I'd rather do it when you're dressed, but if you don't get dressed I'll do it when you're naked."

"Then I thought," my father said, standing, the water running down his body, "that if we fought, maybe it wouldn't be such an uneven match after all." He picked up his shirt and wiped himself off, threw the shirt onto the grass, climbed into his slacks. "You've had a pretty soft life, Dennis. You've never fought for blood. I have."

"Do you think I'm afraid of you?" I asked.

"No," he said. We were standing face to face, and I could see the muscles in his shoulders and chest tensing. "But I'm not afraid of you either."

For a long time neither of us said, did anything. A frog started croaking right by our feet. My father licked his lips. I cleared my throat and said:

"You're going to leave tonight, aren't you?"

He said, "Yes."

"Are you going home?"

"Not right away." He blinked, momentarily bringing back the same vacant expression I used to hate, but then he narrowed his eyes and peered very hard at my face. "If I could figure out a way to hurt you," he said, "I would. You condescend. We're not going to be able to know each other until you realize in what way we're equal."

"Good-bye," I said.

He held out his hand. "Good-bye."

I left my father and walked back to the house. It was beginning to get dark. Maxie had set the table for two, and the absence of the third place oppressed me. I left most of my food. The meat loaf smelled stale, rancid. Maxie cleared the table, carried out the garbage, and screamed. I ran onto the porch. Maxie stood at the rocker, the garbage pail spilled on the ground beside her.

In the garden my father was dragging up pole beans, kicking over cabbages, tearing down tomato plants.

"Aren't you going to do anything?" Maxie wailed.

I leaned against the kitchen door and, ready to welcome hate or the rigid fusing of respect to love, watched my father rage.

Two

The next morning, my father's steps woke me. He was walking back and forth in the room upstairs, where he had slept. When he sat on the bed, the springs sang. Outside the window, the morning was stark and uncomplicated, the low slanting sunlight making the side of the barn and the trees behind it look like an underdeveloped photograph. My father creaked down the stairs, trying not to wake Maxie and me. I lay back in bed and pretended to be asleep. I heard him pass our door. I let him go without saying good-bye. I heard the screen door bang shut.

The night before, Maxie had retreated to our bedroom and I had waited in the kitchen for my father to come in from the garden. But, too ashamed or angry, he had skulked about outside for so long I finally decided he had left, hitchhiking in the dark either back to Springfield or to wherever he intended to travel.

Before going to bed, I had walked upstairs and looked in his room. His suitcase was open on the floor. The few pieces of clothing he had brought hardly covered the suitcase's cardboard bottom. If he had left, it was not much to abandon. I went to sleep, thinking of him walking through the night, skipping around to stick out his thumb whenever a car's headlights flashed on the woods beside the road.

He must have come in late, sneaking upstairs, afraid Maxie would make good on her threat that he couldn't spend the night. But where else could he go? As worn out by the day as we were, he probably was too tired to start trekking down the highway.

I waited a few moments after the screen door slammed, then climbed from bed and went to the window in the other room, which overlooked the road. My father, already to the fork, his sleeves rolled up to his biceps like a laborer, was strolling along, swinging his suitcase and whistling.

I didn't want to look at the garden, not right away. I dressed, left a note for Maxie, and drove into town, bullied by my father's route into taking back roads, half fearing, half hoping I might meet him at the diner, where I stopped for breakfast. I wasted the morning, poking about in stores, looking at magazines, trying on a pair of boots, glancing nervously, hopefully through the store windows at the street whenever anyone of my father's build passed. But I didn't see him.

I kept my dentist's appointment, a little before lunchtime, and drove home. Maxie was on the front porch, waiting for me.

"There's something floating in the well," she said. "I think it's a dog."

Her voice was aggressive, proud of her discovery, and anxious for praise. She had braided her hair into pigtails, which she never does unless she is happy. Finding the animal's corpse made her feel capable.

Ever since we moved to Leverett, the farm had been filled with death. My father's murderous anger seemed a natural way for our garden to die. All that was left was the kohlrabi and salsify—a small row I had tucked in the back corner of the plot behind the Chinese cabbage, an afterthought, curiosities, the vegetable freak show. Salsify could taste like oysters. Kohlrabi felt wonderful to say, like rolling a cherry pit over your tongue, and their pale octopus-bodies sat in the soil like visual puns.

The week before, one of our rabbits had drooped, a doll missing half its stuffing. There was dried blood on its fur the morning we found it dead. Maxie buried the body behind the barn. The next day, we found the earth dug up and the grave empty.

The wind propped open the chickenhouse door, and our rooster vanished. Our cats brought us presents of dead baby moles, which they left in our slippers, and half-dead birds, which fluttered crabwise across our bedroom floor.

The soil, the wild plants, the overripe cucumbers turning bright orange on their broken vines, the rotting tomatoes—some spoiling unpicked on the vine; others torn up by my father, split open and squashed into the dirt—everything breathed out a sweet reek of decay. It was suffocating. I always had thought of autumn as being a metallic season. Leaves bronzing on the branch, the nights iron with cold. In my parents' suburban garden things withered and died brittle.

And our well had gone bad. Maxie shoved a brimful tumbler at my face.

"Smell," she said.

The water stank like rotten lamb, and intrigued me because it hinted at the smell of the dentist's gas—moonair, he had called it—that I had snuffled that morning. The nurse had stuck the gas mask, a rubber Hallowe'en nose, in the center of my face.

"How're you feeling, Dennis?" the dentist asked, and because he knew I could not answer—I felt I was standing at the back of a speeding train, shouting at a figure fast receding into the distance—his question struck me as sinister.

For ten minutes I had wandered across the silent surface of my brain while he probed and drilled. When, exposing a nerve, he triggered pain, the shock lit up my trance like a flare disclosing the hideous presence of a footprint on a dead planet.

Amazed, I had yanked off the gas mask. Their reassuring drone—the doctor: "Just relax" and the nurse: "You just had a bad dream"—terrified me. The music from the dentist's radio was a glass floor that separated me from a plunge into panic. All the way back from Amherst, I had carried this growing horror to test against Maxie. I wanted her concern to leach it out of me. Instead, she met me with her smug discovery.

"Whatever it is," she said, putting the glass down on the table, "it's been floating in the well for days."

The pain in my tooth had grown roots, and the lower left side of my jaw ached. I fished an envelope from my shirt pocket and spilled out a pill, which I dropped on my tongue and swallowed with the offending water.

"What are you doing?" she said. What she meant was: you're not taking me seriously.

If I thought the water safe enough to drink, I was dismissing her morning's work. Her voice carefully moving from word to word as though she were picking her way across a rocky field, she said:

"I tried dragging the body out, but pieces kept coming off. So I turned on all the taps to drain the well. We can clean it out when it's empty."

She was demanding approval. She had coped with a crisis. Somehow it gave her a hold on the farm. But my jaw hurt; I still hadn't shaken my fear of the dentist's office; and the more insistent she became in describing her ingenuity in dealing with the well, the more I felt unnecessary. I didn't have a hold on the farm.

I felt as though I had been living on the tight skin of the land. I hadn't put down roots. When we first moved to Massachusetts, the farm had been a promise; and I felt betrayed. I kept asking something of the place that the place refused to give. I had abandoned a safe future as a city planner, but the land refused to accept me. Maxie, by her own admission, had sacrificed less—she had been uneasy in the grip of any job; but I felt that the farm, having shown her the corpse in the well, had accepted her.

"Ballen's excavating the tooth," I said, following her into the kitchen. "Root canal work. I went crazy under the gas."

Angrily, she scraped carrot shavings from the drainer.

"I felt like everything was speeding up," I said, "like the earth was beginning to spin faster."

"Aren't you going to look at the well?" she asked.

I had ignored her cheerful satisfaction. She would ignore my complaint.

I dumped the rest of the water into the sink, clapped the glass onto the counter, and left to examine the well.

Halfway up the hill to the well stood a sycamore with thick bare branches that now in fall looked like roots snagging the air. Last April, I had wedged a platform onto the shoulder of the largest bough; but, every time the tree shrugged in the wind, the boards loosened. When I had abandoned the tree, two boys from the neighboring farm invaded and, by using some stubborn magic, locked the planks in place.

Like a mutt circling round and round on a rug, hunting for a snug spot in which to curl, I prowled all summer—through the woods, through the barn, through the house. Every place I sat seemed to straddle an angle.

I was a nester. Only the solid, the motionless, and the fixed guaranteed a sensible world. I wanted everything labeled and under glass, immobile, so if I went away I could be sure of the landscape when I returned. I tended to make whatever possessions I had into artifacts, useless except as exhibits of my activities. Something that is used can be misplaced; and the fear of loss, like an unexplainable tapping in the wall, haunted me. In a nightmare that had dogged me since childhood, I would dream that I had awakened in an alien room and that the steps I heard coming down the hall were made by my parents, who however would be as strange as the place—they would have gills, or flowers instead of eyes, or lipless mouths.

When I was seven, I once on roller skates sailed over the hump of a street and plunged whizzing down the steep slope. There was a moment just before rounding the top when I knew that I was about to shoot down the hill out of control and that there was no way I could prevent it. Then there was a smear of lawn, tree, car, hydrant . . .

I wanted everything to freeze for a second. Just to catch my breath, to glance around, to prepare for the speed, and to accept the chance pleasure or to resist the rush of terror.

Maxie on the other hand was a gypsy. Motion constantly rearranged her world; and she, as though staring through a kaleidoscope, delighted in the continual change. All she needed was one still seat in the heart of the stir.

She discovered the back stairs' landing where she built a window seat and a ladder of narrow shelves. She refused all help and hammered sullenly, clutching the six-penny nails as though they were a fistful of worms about to slither through her fingers. When I remarked, during a pause in her work, that her hands were red-pocked where the nails had gouged, she slammed from the kitchen.

She was trying to subdue the house by herself and was jealous of whatever success she was having; although, when I avoided the back stairs, her work became abruptly noisy. Alone, she would swear and slam things with increasing viciousness and frequency until I would wander up to sit on the steps above her, silently watching. She wanted a witness to her triumph. However, if the cheap pine split or the wall mysteriously mutated from wood to metal, bending nails whose points skidded along a scratch of sparks, she would chase me away; and I would sit in the kitchen by the Ashley stove, reading, until the banging began again.

But, after a week's struggle, she made her peace. She accepted separated seams; bent nails that, hammered into the wood, looked like dark larvae; skewed angles. And the house accepted her.

Once I sat, uncomfortable, in her windowseat on her green coach blanket, which, because of the sinking afternoon sun that slid bars of light across the thick nap, seemed like a pool of water beneath me. I leafed through *The King's Stilts,* a rain-warped copy of *Ozma Of Oz,* old *National Geographics,* exploring Maxie's childhood as though it were an exotic country, described and pictured in the yellowing pages. *Old Dutch Nursery Rhymes,* an ancient volume with pale exact pictures that looked as glossy as egg albumen, was her oldest book.

When she found me reading it, she turned to the song "In Holland Stands A House," which she explained had been her childhood favorite. Tentatively, as though building a card tower, she sang:

> *In Holland stands a house,*
> *In Holland stands a house,*
> *Heigh-O, jig jigety, ting-a-ling,*
> *Join hands together and form a ring . . .*

Each verse peopled the house with another member of the family:

> *The man he has a wife,*
> *The wife she has a child,*
> *The child it has a maid . . .*

"The song was like a plastic shmoo I once had," Maxie said. "Every time you opened one of the shmoos, you found a smaller one inside. It seemed to go on forever."

The descending relationships of possession irked me.

> *The maid she has a boy,*
> *The boy he has a dog . . .*

Part of my decision to move to the country had been to escape from that feeling of contracting space. I didn't want to be enclosed. Our farm, bounded on two sides by undeveloped woods, gave me a temporary pocket that, like a bubble of air in a sinking car, was slowly shrinking. My magic circle was becoming a noose.

Maxie had found her place; but, because it excluded me, I resented the space it filled. As she stood owning the landing and more and more surely seizing the notes of the song, I felt both betrayed and in sympathy with her betrayal. It was as though we were both trapped in that sinking car, sharing that air bubble; and she, in a vigorous effort to save herself—to wriggle out a window or to squeeze through a partially opened door—was using up the oxygen.

> *Now the boy turns out the dog,*
> *And the maid sends off the boy,*
> *And the wife sends off the maid* . . .

The last verses, which for her, she said, evoked the comfortable snap of closure, opened up for me an abysmal inevitability. Fate constantly was nudging us down a narrowing tunnel at the end of which was an opening into the pure empty light of some promised afterlife—that we can never reach because the too-small bottleneck traps us. All we can do is lie still.

> *And the wife now leaves the house,*
> *And the man must leave it too,*
> *And the house now catches fire,*
> *And the child is left alone.*

The pain in my tooth had begun to vanish like the point on our television screen that, after the picture has been snapped off, shrinks into itself and then, having paused, leaps into the black. Because I distrust pills, I was sure that somewhere inside me the pain still lurked; and the suspicion that something not me was sharing my skull rooted itself into my imagination. I felt as uncomfortable in my body as I did in the house, as uncomfortable as I did on the farm.

I was a temporary boarder. I was lodged in my flesh as insecurely as my platform had been set in the sycamore. A good breeze could shake me free.

At the top of the hill, I lifted the planks that covered the mouth of the well and propped them against a tree. Inside the well, floating in the black and oily-looking water, was the dog's corpse. Skaters jerked back and forth across the surface, leaving a trail of overlapping concentric rings. I gagged on the smell—like burned liver—that wafted from the hole.

Stepping back to clear my nostrils and throat, I tripped over one of the propped boards and grabbed a branch to keep from falling down the slope. Below me, at the bottom of a deep basin, lay the farm: the ruined garden, the collapsing barn, and the house, which in the late light appeared painted not white but orange. Everything looked odd. It was as though Maxie, having made the land her home, had altered the landscape. For a moment, I—on skates and seven again—was rolling over the rim of my childhood hill. What had been terrifying me all that day, ever since my father left, was this promise of appalling acceleration.

As I walked down the hill to the house, there was a roar behind the barn; and Maxie came around the silo pushing the gasoline lawn mower as though it were a baby carriage carrying a monstrous infant with dragon lungs. All summer, we had argued about cutting the grass. I liked the wild growth that swallowed Maxie's red baseball cap, and a whiffleball we bought one afternoon during an exuberant, commodity-crazed romp through a discount department store, and a screwdriver I carefully had laid on an old wool shirt while I was tuning our asthmatic Volkswagen, and my left sandal, which must have hopped from our kitchen porch where, after coming back from a spring evening swim, I had tossed it with its mate. I liked stepping blindly on a plastic blue brontosaurus or an orange crocodile or a khaki GI Joe, fragments of a toy universe left behind by earlier tenants of our farm. The row of animals and soldiers on our living room windowsill lengthened with summer until the middle of August when, in addition to the lawn's surprises, we began to discover the things we had lost in the past year: the cap, torn and pink; the whiffleball, cracked; my sandal, warped and chewed; the screwdriver, rusted—treasures that I put on the windowsill with the beasts and infantrymen, trying to connect our life with the lives of those who had lived here before us. This game of lost and found was one of my strategies for making myself at home. The wilderness of the uncut lawn reflected comfortingly my own wildness.

For Maxie, mowing the lawn was part of the proper arrangement of life. Raking the cut blades of grass gave her the same satisfaction as peeling a sunburn or flaying an old sofa that she had condemned to be reupholstered with vivid modern cloth. Even paring a peach left her feeling stripped clean as though she were the peach and her skin were a dust cover protecting her sterile flesh. She liked moving with the mower in the core of the racket and the stench, wrapped in the blue oily exhaust like some goddess of industry with fire in her belly and flames licking from her eyes.

Seeing me, she paused. Lifting her right foot to scratch an ankle speckled with bits of grass, she shouted, with exaggerated pouts and grimaces, something that was inaudible because of the mower's din.

"I can't hear you," I shouted back.

She thrust her head forward and furrowed her brow while her mouth slipped from a kiss to a grin as she—I think—asked, "What?"

We played charades for a few minutes, she unwilling to kill the motor and I—feeling that by cutting the grass, she was trying to sever my fragile connection with the farm—refusing to approach close enough to hear her over the motor's noise. She trundled the mower toward me; and, leaning over the handlebar, her face blotched with pink, her cheeks coated with sweat and black speckles, she shouted, "Your mother called. She wants you to go to Springfield."

"Does she want me to call back?" I shouted.

"She wants you to go," Maxie shouted. "She's upset about your father."

"What does she expect me to do?" I shouted.

"What?" Maxie shouted.

"I don't want to get caught in the middle," I shouted.

"She needs you," Maxie shouted.

"I'm not going," I shouted.

"What?" Maxie shouted.

"I'm not going," I shouted. "Turn that off."

"What will you do," Maxie shouted, "when *I* need you?"

"You're not my mother," I shouted.

"What?" Maxie shouted.

"Turn that off," I shouted and, bending, tripped the kill switch.

The motor unwound its roar until all that was left was a whistle. It coughed and, after a long pause, coughed again like an intruder who, having stumbled onto a domestic quarrel, wants politely to announce his presence.

Tears rolled down both sides of Maxie's nose and along her cheeks, leaving on her dirty skin clean streaks, which looked pasty and raised like scars.

"I'm going for a ride," I said.

As I backed the car down the driveway, Maxie, hunched over, her back heaving from her sobs, was rewinding the mower's starter rope around the flywheel's rim.

I drove around and around Leverett in a vicious widening circle, searching through the sudden drizzle, which had lain in wait for me behind a low blue hill, for a snug spot where I could park and brood. The inside of the car smelled like soiled socks. The windshield wipers, like a team of monotonous vaudevillians, did their dull dance until I was dizzy. I nudged the car up a rutted road and stopped beside the control shack overlooking the public dump, which, with its spiral packed-dirt path descending around the circumference of a neat deep pit, looked more like an amphitheater than a scientific landfill. At the center of the hollow, where a stage would have been, a scanty mound of garbage, topped by a soggy mattress, smoldered.

On Saturday afternoons, when I was a child, my father and I used to drive the week's accumulation of trash to the dump in Longmeadow, Springfield's wealthy suburb on the other side of Forest Park. After emptying the barrels we had brought, my father liked to root through the dump for anything—radios with cracked cases, wobbly rocking chairs, a brass eagle with one chipped wing—that was still serviceable. Everything he found proved to him capitalism's corruption.

"Look what the rich throw away," he said one day, digging a rusty bicycle with bent wheel rims from under old bedsprings and bags of tin cans. "It wouldn't be too hard to fix up. Should we take it home?"

When we unloaded our prize from the car's trunk, my mother, standing on the back porch, her wet hands raised half in a shrug and half in an appeal, soapsuds rolling down her forearms and dripping from her bony elbows, railed at my father for dragging home junk.

"I'm going to fix it this afternoon," my father said as he carted the broken bicycle to the garage; and, using me to deflect or absorb my mother's anger, he added, "Dennis needs a bicycle."

"He doesn't need one right now," my mother said, "do you, Dennis?"

The question was not rhetorical. My mother wanted a declaration of loyalty. She demanded precedence in my affections. She wooed and bullied me into denying my father.

"He'd rather have a new one," she coaxed. "Wouldn't you?"

"Yeah," I said, "I guess so . . ."

"Anyway," she said, "that bicycle's a complete wreck."

"All it needs," my father said, "is an hour's work."

But that hour was elusive; and my father's treasures,

like the stuff I uncovered in our farm's overgrown grass, accumulated unused. What charmed him was not repairing and not hoarding, but the initial rescue. In my game of lost and found, I was mimicking my father and tempting Maxie into my mother's role, which is why her cutting the grass had angered me. She was playing her part too well. I wanted to restage my parents' conflicts and, by resolving them differently, in some occult way change their relationship and free myself from the model of marriage they had willed me. But, by trying to escape their influence, I was courting a sad repetition of their behavior, a repetition that terrified me because it seemed fated, stamped on my genes as though it were part of some cellular baggage lugged down the ages. As in a hall of mirrors, each generation reflects the generation before which in turn reflects the generation before. It's all the same; nothing changes. Every time a woman spreads her thighs to give birth, her womb becomes a tunnel, leading back to the first shiver, which sent life barreling through the centuries.

I didn't want to go to Springfield. I suspected my mother's appeal was not for support in a crisis, but for a show of solidarity. She wanted to isolate my father in the same way that she used to, by making his schemes seem so foolish that neither my sister nor I could defend him.

And he didn't need to be defended. By trying to protect him, I would be suggesting that he was too weak or too cowardly to protect himself, which is what my mother believed.

"He never was a strong man," she once told me.

"He's afraid to say no. He'll do anything anyone asks him to do."

"He's generous," I said, not sure I was right.

"He doesn't know his own mind," she said.

By running away, he demonstrated that he did know what he wanted: he wanted space. Despite what he had written in his letter to me, he had said, the first night he was in Leverett, "When I was in the Home, sometimes I'd wake up in the middle of the night and listen to everybody in the dormitory beds around me breathing in their sleep. I was sure they were using up all the air. I'd start gasping, afraid I was suffocating. Ever since last spring, that's begun happening again. I wake in the middle of the night, and I can't breathe."

"When we first got married," my mother once said, "he used to scream at night. He had terrible dreams. He said he's always done that, ever since he was a boy. After you were born, he never woke up screaming again."

The glimpse of my father screaming at night, which my mother had given me—an image I could not superimpose over my father's calm daytime face— seemed, as I grew older, to be something I had imagined, not something real I had been told. Afraid to ask my mother outright if my memory of her statement was correct—"Did Dad really used to wake up screaming?"—I weighted the image down with examples of his silliness (silly men don't wake up screaming) and sank it in some psychic backwater. My mother was right: there were many times when my father was foolish. Once my father took my sister and me on an outing in Boston to the Maparium (a huge glass globe that looked like a spherical stained-glass window) in the Christian Science Monitor Building. I walked across the bridge, which cored through the center of that globe, and gazed at the vivid orange, blue, and red countries encircling me. The glass was lit from behind and the translucent hemispheres above and below seemed, in their fragility, to promise an equally fragile planet on which humans lived and reproduced.

I was ten years old and only recently had discovered atomic bombs, which had taken an immediate and dominant position in the hierarchy of things to be scared of. At night, I would listen to the distant planes rumbling overhead, which sounded like God clearing His throat; and I would wait for the flash of light and the blast I knew was due. As I leaned over the bridge inside the glass globe, I imagined what would happen if I suddenly slipped and plunged the twenty or so feet to the continent that lay below me. I could, if I fell, shatter South America and send cracks spiderwebbing through North America, the Antarctic, and both the Atlantic and Pacific oceans. In this fancy, I became the Bomb that could destroy the earth. Huge chunks of Venezuela, Brazil, and Peru, like the jagged polygons of a smashed egg-shell, would litter the floor below the globe.

If there were a floor below the globe.

What if the globe hung suspended, not in the Christian Science Monitor Building, but in a vacuum, and, once it were shattered, all that would be revealed was an emptiness as blank and as unrelieved as a movie screen before the show starts? I closed my eyes. I was nauseated by the vertiginous idea of falling forever through space while above me the broken earth grew smaller and smaller—the size of a basketball, then of a baseball, then of a quarter, then of a pinhead—until that one reference point had vanished and I no longer could tell if I were falling or were merely floating.

I had just read *Alice In Wonderland,* and this drop from one world into another seemed, despite its terrors, also an escape. I stared at the colored-glass continents below me, meditating on bombs and falling bodies, until my father, who had a severe headache, put a hand on my shoulder and steered me out of the Maparium and into a vast, dusty, wax-smelling hall, where he stopped at a desk to ask in a loud voice for an aspirin.

I don't recall if I knew enough about Christian Science then to be humiliated or if my wince came, delayed, years later. But for a long time, through the cruelly judgmental years of high school and college, that moment in the Christian Science Monitor Building seemed to be most typical of my father.

The lady behind the desk glared at my father and then looked down at her blotter. My father, thinking she may not have heard him, asked in a louder voice for aspirin. She stared even more intently at her blotter, her hands flat on its moss-green nap, one index finger nervously rubbing back and forth, rolling up a small dark string of blotter fibers until she had worn away a hole. My father, not impatient—he rarely showed impatience—but curious about why he was not getting a response, started using hand signs, pantomiming opening an aspirin tin, turning on a faucet, getting a glass of water, turning off a faucet, putting a pill on his tongue, and swallowing. The Christian Scientist ducked her head even lower, her cheeks getting red. She was sure my father was making fun of her beliefs.

My father sighed and scratched his cheek. How come she wasn't responding? he wondered. He took out a pen and notebook and wrote: "Do you have any aspirin I could have?" He put the piece of paper in the center of the blotter. "Aspirin," he shouted, pointing at his mouth. "Aspirin."

The poor woman began to weep. Tears trickled down her cheeks and dripped onto the blotter, leaving black spots, which sent out thread-like rays as the blotter absorbed. My father stared at the spotted blotter, amazed and disconcerted at the—to him—inexplicable show of emotion. As we left the building without having gotten any aspirin, my father, inventing an explanation for the puzzling display, said, "She must be having trouble at home."

How could a man innocent enough to ask a Christian Scientist for aspirin wake up screaming at night? I wondered. I ignored all evidence of seriousness because he never lost his temper, and I suppose I equated—and still may do so—seriousness with anger. I wanted to believe he was a silly man, but he wasn't.

Some years after he moved to Springfield, he started agitating for a teachers' union. The union that existed was—he claimed—a company union, which never disagreed with the School Committee. It was called the Springfield Educational Association, the SEA, which to the naive eye and ear of a child spelled *sea,* so I always imagined the SEA to be an oceanic force, which my father—like King Canute on the beach—was trying to stop. He seemed heroic, but even his heroism seemed a little foolish.

To call attention to the demands he thought a real union should make—better wages, better retirement and medical benefits, a better life insurance plan—my father launched a strike all by himself. It was a curiously gentle strike. My father did not want to deprive his students of an education, an education he felt he was best equipped to give them, so he limited his picketing to after-school hours.

When the final bell rang, he would take off his suit jacket and put on a heavy plaid wool shirt, the kind construction workers wore; and he would march up and down in front of the high school where he taught, carrying a sign that listed his grievances. He crunched through the drifts of dried leaves. He called to the people looking sideways out the windows of their cars, which they slowed as they passed him. He stood, bouncing from one foot to the other—like a boxer in training—to keep warm; and he argued with the hecklers who surrounded and baited him. A few of his students, unsure whether to jeer or defer to him, paused to watch and listen; and my father with quick impatient gestures waved them closer and, trying to be fair, explained, not only his position, but the antagonistic position of the SEA and the School Committee. The boys, their blue notebooks held stiff-armed close to their thighs, and the girls, their notebooks pressed like shields against their breasts, asked no questions of him, but snickered and murmured to each other while my father lectured.

I was eleven, and I begged to be allowed to picket with him. He made a sandwich board for me out of shirt cardboards taped together, which said: "Teachers have families to support too" on one side and "Support the AFT"—the American Federation of Teachers, the local branch of which my father was trying to start—on the other. While my father harangued the crowd, I stood beside him, glancing from one unfriendly face to another. We stayed out until twilight. As we walked home together, our placards rolled under our arms, the streetlamps came on, very yellow in the dusk. I used the excuse of a chill to turn up my jacket collar as hoodlums did. My father, as silent with me as he was voluble with his students and the crowd of curiosity-seekers, hunched his shoulders against the cold, which gave his shadow humps on each side of his head, making it look like the shadow of a large bird with folded wings. When we reached our house, which was at the top of a hill, my father stopped and turned, looking down at the city cupped in the river valley below us; and, breaking his silence, he gestured down the slope and asked, "Think you can beat me to the end of the block?"

We sprinted the few hundred feet to the curb. The lights of the city and, beyond the city, the bridges over the wide Connecticut River and, on the other shore, West Springfield glimmered in the autumn dark. The smell of the night was as clear, as chilly, and as sharp as glass needles in the nostrils, painfully pure. The race—which we often ran after coming home from picketing—became our ritual, a moment shared before we went inside to the bright, supper-smelling house. Despite his limp, my father could run fast. He always beat me, always said, as we huffed back up the block home, that he was getting old and it wouldn't be too long before I beat him.

Two or three times a week, after supper, my father's cronies stopped by the house to play jazz and argue politics. Frank Polishook, a Polish science teacher, was as short as my father, but bulkier. He had grown up on a farm outside Springfield and still had a tough farm boy's muscles, which bulged on his forearms and upper arms like wet twisted towels. Polishook was an anarchist, who had hewed a bomb shelter out of the granite bedrock on which he had built his house. The shelter, a damp dim chamber that smelled like stagnant pond water, had a table, a few kerosene lanterns, and dozens of cartons of canned goods. When my father took me to visit Polishook and see the shelter, we sat, listening to the breeze blow across the door with the low whistle of someone blowing across the top of a soda bottle, while Polishook described the improvements he intended to make: air filter, generator, paneling, wooden floor, chemical toilet. The room was twelve feet by fourteen feet.

"I'd rather blow up," my father said.

"I'm going to put a chess board down here," Polishook said. "And books."

By the end of the fifties, Polishook had become a John Birchite, his anarchism leading him down an alley of self-interest. His shelter, which had been enlarged and elaborated, looked like a den. It had knotty-pine walls, an oak floor, acoustical tiles on the ceiling, a bar, a generator-powered refrigerator in which he kept bottles of Polish vodka mixed with sweet raspberry syrup, a pool table, a rack of rifles, and—as he had promised my father—a chess set and a library, which included *The Encyclopaedia Britannica, The Book of Knowledge, The Harvard Classics,* and bound back issues of *Popular Mechanics, Popular Science,* and *Field & Stream.* He had installed a wood-burning furnace and painted it to look like the whale in Walt Disney's cartoon film *Pinocchio.* Little by little, he had bought all the land surrounding his house, so finally he owned an entire mountain of five hundred acres, on which he hunted deer. On weekends, he lived in his bomb shelter and cooked his venison on a propane stove while listening to his shortwave radio.

Johnny Butter, a history teacher, who wore knicker-bockers and drove a Packard, also stopped at our house after supper. He was a Trotskyite, whose ancestors had followed William Pynchon from Roxbury, Massachusetts, to Springfield in 1636. He lived on Crescent Hill in a Victorian mansion that was always dark because he refused to use any but forty-watt bulbs in his light fixtures. He thought brighter bulbs were wasteful. Very thin and very tall, he habitually stooped, his body forming a question mark, and his expression was puzzled, as though the question he punctuated could not be answered. He claimed to be physiologically unable to cry; his tear ducts did not function normally. As a result, whenever he was sad enough to weep, he would suffer extreme pain. During the twenty years my father knew him, Butter spent a great deal of time and money going to specialists who promised to cure his ailment, to let him cry.

Polishook and Butter, like the others who visited— the Henry Wallace Democrats, the Stalinists, the DeLeon and Norman Thomas Socialists, the old Wobblies—refused at first to support my father's efforts to start a union until it was decided what politics the union would adhere to. My father, a pluralist, wanted to include every political sect, Republicans as well as pro-Soviets. He did not believe in any kind of closed shop. He did not even want the union, if it became successful, to have a stranglehold on the teaching community.

The teachers would drink and rant at each other, while my mother herded my sister and me into my father's study upstairs on the second floor. Halfway through the evening, when the arguing devolved into personal attacks, or, occasionally, thrown punches and broken furniture, my father would take out his trumpet and start playing one of the old jazz tunes he knew. Polishook sat at the piano, the stool pushed far back, his arms straight out as though he were about to swan-dive into the keys, his fingers amazingly nimble. Butter dragged his drums from the trunk of his car and, having set them up in front of the fireplace, played leaning far forward, his head turned, his ear next to the skins, his eyes closed. The other teachers retrieved their instruments from the front hall where they left them when they came in, or sat—the ones who didn't play instruments—tapping their feet and humming or singing along. My sister and I would slip downstairs to sprawl on the floor, eating pretzels and gulping beer from forgotten opened bottles.

Of the leftists who congregated at my parents' house, Polishook and Butter were the first to overcome their objections to the new union; and they joined out of affection for my father, not because they agreed with his tactics or politics. But Polishook and Butter—local characters—were popular at their schools, and they were obstinate. They dogged their co-workers through the halls and hounded them at faculty meetings. One by one, they signed them up. The union grew, and although it was still small compared to the SEA, the School Committee became nervous.

To discredit my father and destroy his union, the School Committee asked the F.B.I. to investigate him. The F.B.I., grandstanding in order to disgrace my father in front of his students—who, they were afraid, might have been politically infected by his radical ideas—came to my father's class during school hours to ask him to go with them for questioning.

When the agents arrived in his classroom, my father was dressed in a shoulder-length white wig, spirit-gummed mustache and beard, and a ratty gray caftan. His face was made up as sallow as a bruise, and he had puttied his large nose to make it larger. As was his custom, my father was acting out a scene from Shakespeare, trying to demonstrate to his students that the plays were stories to watch, not merely texts to read. He was, that day, teaching *The Merchant of Venice*; he was disguised as Shylock.

The F.B.I. agents took my father to an office across

from the City Hall and next door to the Court Square Theater, which alternated movies with vaudeville. "As they questioned me," my father told us, "I looked out the window at the alley where someone was walking greyhounds from an act. He'd come out the door with a greyhound on a leash, stroll up and down a few times, and then go back in. A few minutes later, he'd come out the door again with, I assume, another greyhound on a leash, walk him up and down, and go back in. A few minutes later, he'd come out with another dog, walk him, and go back in. This went on for the hour I was in the office. I don't know why he didn't walk them all at once."

The F.B.I. questioning was designed simply to give the School Committee an excuse to fire my father. This was during the early McCarthy years. My father sued the School Committee for reinstatement, arguing in open letters to the city's two newspapers that anyone who understood politics knew that the socialist party to which he belonged was more anti-Soviet than the House Un-American Activities Committee. Russia had betrayed the Revolution. He couldn't forgive that. He demanded that J. Edgar Hoover run a real investigation on him and make the findings public. He had nothing to be afraid or ashamed of in his past.

Having noticed how disarmed the F.B.I. agents had been by his Shylock costume when they arrested him (my father had refused to take the disguise off; he had classes to teach all day and it would have taken him too long to get back in costume after the questioning), my father found a lawyer who agreed to put him on the stand dressed as Marx, Engels, Lenin, Trotsky, and Stalin, and to let my father expound upon the differences among the various socialist and communist dogmas. My father wanted publicity because he saw the trial as a chance to educate the public politically. He had faith in his neighbors.

The judge, a man named Conor with a red raised birthmark disfiguring half his face, was a Catholic. Having been educated by the Jesuits, he admired my father's logical mind as much as he deplored his politics. He allowed the trial to run its flamboyant course, patiently allowing my father to make his case, while he sat with his elbow on his chair arm and his birthmarked cheek resting, hidden, in his upraised hand.

The last day of the trial was the first day it snowed that year. My father stopped in the middle of his speech and, crossing to the window, said simply, "Look, it's snowing. It's too beautiful a day to talk any more politics."

It was a beautiful day. The snow, caught against the mullions of the high windows, spread across the glass, making the room darker. The radiators hissed, thin filaments of steam spraying from the valves. The courtroom seemed more closed, cozier. Sounds—spectators' coughs, the rustle of papers as lawyers shuffled their notes—seemed louder. My father thanked the court, the jury, and the visitors for bearing with him and sat down abruptly. He was not in costume. It was his day to address the jury as himself. But he fingered his cheek as though he were trying to tug off some final mask of flesh, as though the teacher who was fighting for his job was as much a disguise as the radical leaders he had been impersonating.

The judge cleared his throat in the quiet, sat up straight in his squeaking chair, and said, "Yes, it is a beautiful day outside." He called a lunch recess.

Later, after the trial was over, one of the jurors admitted to a friend that she had been charmed by my father's sudden interruption of his speech to comment on the weather. That had decided her to vote in his favor. The rumor piggybacked its way on one conversation after another until it reached my father, who said, "I thought so. When Emily Dickinson was at Mount Holyoke College, she once wrote on a test paper that it was too beautiful a day to be in class and left. She got an 'A.'"

The jury found for my father. The judge, after the trial was over, paused in the doorway of his chambers and, getting my father's attention with a crook of his finger, quoted St. Augustine: "Bear with me, my God, while I say something of my wit, Thy gift, and on what dotage I wasted it."

My father, who had not memorized any St. Augustine, but, after eleven years in college, had memorized some Horace, responded in Latin: "*Adhuc sub judice lis est,*" which means "The proceedings are still in front of the judge" or, more colloquially, "The jury's still out on that." My father did not believe he was wasting his intelligence on unworthy doctrines.

Although my father won his case, the publicity had marked our family. The week after the trial ended, I was stopped on my way home from school by three neighborhood kids who beat me up, cracking a tooth. They ran off, laughing and throwing snowballs at each other. I sat on the icy sidewalk, legs splayed out in front of me, looking for my glasses. They had been knocked into a snowbank, and their impression in the snow, a little skewed, looked like a shadow of a pair of glasses. I dug them out, smeared snow from the lenses, and put them on. But I could not see through them, so I took them off, folded them, and fumbled them into my jacket pocket. I put a handful of snow up to my swollen lip, held it there until the pain of the cold made me take it away, and gazed dumbly at the bright red blood that had soaked into the snow. A car skidding at the end of the street cast zigzagging light on the fronts of houses, trees, parked cars. I unsteadily stood, zipped up my jacket to my chin, and walked slowly home.

When my mother asked, "What happened to you?" I told her I had tripped and fallen down.

"Where?" she asked.

She had been making soup and the kitchen was steamy. Ice had formed on the inside of the windows. I scratched at it with my thumbail. My father, seeing my embarrassment and suspecting what had happened, said, "You've got to learn how to keep yourself from tripping."

A week later, the same three kids stopped me as I was walking up the block to our house. One of them, a moon-faced boy with a vertical crease at the tip of his nose, which made his nose look like a chin, said, "Isn't your father a commie-traitor?"

When I swung at him, I felt a tap at the back of my neck, and it seemed someone had clapped a gloved hand over my eyes. I blinked. I was kneeling on the sidewalk. My right pantleg was ripped. My knee was bloody. The moon-faced kid was jiggling a bicycle chain, which he had just used to crack me on the back of the head.

I heard my father saying something. Standing in his shirtsleeves on the front porch, he was calling to the three kids who were circled around me. He didn't sound angry. He sounded stern, but fair, like a referee at a sports event.

"Three against one," he said. "You afraid to fight one-on-one?"

The kids edged away from me, ready to bolt down the street. To keep from frightening them off, my father sat on our porch steps.

"In my day," he said, "only cowards fought three against one."

"Commie," the moon-faced boy shouted without conviction.

"I'd rather be red than yellow," said my father.

"I'll fight him," said the moon-faced boy.

I stood, both happy and unhappy that my father had not scattered the kids.

"Take off your glasses," said the moon-faced boy.

I did. We faced each other. The two other kids backed up to give us room. The moon-faced boy chopped at the ice on the sidewalk with his heel. A light snow started to drift down.

My mother came out on the porch, pulling a sweater over her blouse and saying to my father, "Why don't you stop it? Dennis'll get hurt."

"Go inside," said my father.

My mother stared at my father, looked at me and the moon-faced boy—we were both chopping at the ice to give us an arena in which we wouldn't slip—and then she sat down on the porch steps next to my father. She had left the front door open. I could see, inside the house, the familiar bookcase and mirror in the front hall and the bottom part of the stairs.

"Come on," said my father. "It's getting late."

The moon-faced boy and I squared off. He punched me in the face; my nose stung and my eyes watered and I felt like sneezing. I hit him in the side of the head. He hit me in the belly. I hit him in the shoulder and, turning sideways to avoid his swing, hit him in the face. He sat down hard. I jumped on him, bowling him over, and, grabbing his head, started banging it on the sidewalk. He squirmed and kicked, but couldn't shake me.

I felt someone dragging me off. Thinking it was one of his pals, I turned and swung wildly, hitting my father in the gut. He made a sound, half grunt, half laugh, and said, "You're not supposed to kill him."

I was furious. I had won in a fair fight. My father had no right to break it up. I stood, gulping and breathing hard, my shoulders heaving, waiting for the moon-faced boy to stand up, so we could start fighting again. He lay on the sidewalk, his knees pulled up to his belly, his elbows tight against his sides, blinking up at my father. Amazed, I saw a tear pool in the corner of one of his eyes.

"It's time for everyone to go home," said my father.

On the back porch of our farmhouse in Leverett, I caught a whiff of mulled cider: apples, cinnamon, cloves, nutmeg, a homey smell that always evokes

Like Father | 64

in me a sentimental tranquillity that I associate with the nineteenth century and my early childhood and that links the two times, as though the years between 1800 and 1900 had been merely a stage in my development, really existing between 1945 and 1955. On the kitchen stove, forgotten by Maxie, a scum of spiced cider was sizzling on the bottom of a chipped white saucepan. I turned off the gas and went looking for her.

She was in the bathroom, standing with one foot in a red plastic tub on the floor and the other foot propped on the seat of the toilet, giving herself a sponge bath. The kerosene lantern on the toilet tank cast her awkward shadow along the linoleum, up the wall, which, whitewashed, looked like crinkled elephant hide, and onto the ceiling. The undersides of her chin, arms, breasts, and raised leg glistened, wet and orange, as though she had smeared parts of herself with Dayglo paint. The cider in her glass, untouched, had formed a cinnamon-speckled skin.

"I'll go to the spring to get more water tomorrow," she said. "Will you finish cleaning the well?"

"Tomorrow," I said, "let's go to Springfield."

Three

My mother, the day after my father abandoned her, drove a "For Sale" sign into their shaggy front lawn, quit her job as a social worker at the Springfield Geriatric Health Center, and started planning a trip around the world. She tacked maps to every wall and, with a red felt-tipped marker, circled the cities she intended to visit. With a blue marker, she traced her possible path from west to east. The line looped back and forth across the world like ribbon candy. From old *National Geographic* and *Life* magazines, she snipped photographs of foreign cities, which she taped next to the maps, and she stretched green yarn between the pictures and the places they represented.

She stuffed trunks full of clothes and rummaged through thirty years' accumulation of property. In the center of each room, she put a large trash carton; but she couldn't bear to dump anything. She emptied closets, bureaus, bookcases, desks, and stacked the stuff along baseboards.

When Maxie and I arrived at three o'clock in the afternoon, lamps were lit all over the house. For years, my mother had followed the rest of us up and down stairs, switching off lights. The kitchen radio had been left on. A bundle of dirty laundry, wrapped in a clean blue sheet, lay in the hall. Used coffee cups perched on windowsills, the sofa arm, the edge of the coffee table. The television was on although its sound was turned off: two women in a commercial gossiped in an immaculate kitchen.

My mother sat on a red hassock in the living room, looking like a Buddha, sexless and serene. She was digging papers, pictures, old report cards from a split cardboard box, tossing an occasional letter into the fireplace behind her, sorting the rest of the clutter on the living room rug. Collier's *New Photographic History of the World War,* a warped book without a cover: Kerensky sits on a sofa reading a newspaper that is pure light; Lenin with a full beard stands in a garden clutching a fedora by the brim. My great-grandparents, dressed in suits I'm sure they did not own, posed in a framed photograph which lay next to the book. Bundles of letters bound by blackened rubber bands. Back issues of *The Western Socialist,* containing articles my father had written. The piles radiated out from her as though she were the heart of a star.

When Maxie and I entered, she rose with an awkward lumbering lift, her hands pushing against her thighs, and her head bowed. A tired woman with loose translucent skin hanging from her arms as though she were growing rudimentary wings. She had gotten old abruptly. At forty-five, she still had moved casually, had sat without first glancing back at the chair, had struck a match while reading the newspaper. At fifty-five, every action was deliberate. Before she crossed the room, she examined the floor and planned her route.

For her, growing old meant groping more and more blindly in a world that kept slithering from her grasp. She had been proud of her steady hands. When I was in high school, she once received by mail a needle threader, a diamond-shaped tin tongue joined point-to-point to a diamond-shaped wire loop. You slipped the loop into the needle's eye and, having passed the thread into the loop, pulled the loop back through. My mother scorned the threader, but my sister loved it. They staged a needle-threading contest, which my mother easily won—two motions to Hannah's three. My mother, who ever since she had been in a community center production of *The Adding Machine* was a foe of technology, saw her success as a triumph over science.

My father had bought her a dishwasher, which she hated and did not use. When a soapy plate would slip from her hands and shatter on the kitchen floor, she sadly would address the fragments with "I'm growing old." But the way she braced herself before the smash and the terrible pause she would take before sweeping up the shards betrayed more fear than sadness.

My mother's life, as she grew older, as she moved more slowly, seemed a fabric of pauses, like the vests she began crocheting for herself and constantly wearing: blue, green, violet, spaces webbed together by wide cross-hatchings of yarn, as though she were draping herself in nets to keep herself from escaping. She saw herself still as the young social worker who had married my father, as though in marrying she had entered a paradise in which she would never age. And her growing resentment—at my father and at their life together—may have come from her feelings of betrayal: marriage had not kept her from getting old.

After I left for college, although usually my mother hated long phone calls, she would telephone some afternoons to tell me stories about what had happened on a particular case when she was working in one of the poor sections of Providence before she met my father. The people she talked about, in time, became vivid; they took on the attributes of mythological characters who had roamed the earth in a more innocent age: Barry Bissell, who lived in a one-room apartment that stank of unwashed clothes and undumped garbage and who claimed his children had cheated him out of a fortune in savings; Edna Lowery, who carpeted her floor with newspapers because she could not box-train her dozens of cats; the General, who kept a map of Europe open on a table and replayed a battle from World War I over and over as though, alchemically, by changing the outcome of the fight from an Allied disaster to an Allied victory, he could change the past and save the brother who had been killed in that massacre. "The General" was my mother's pet name for him; because he was myopic and had a bad back, he had not gone to Europe to fight. Once, when my mother accidentally bumped the table, upsetting his troops, he made the sign of the cross over her head and prayed God to forgive her.

My mother did not realize that her passion for telling me about her former social work clients seemed as odd to me as their behavior had seemed years ago to her.

Between the time she stood and the time she spoke, she made another of those pauses, a silence so private it seemed an assault for Maxie or me to speak. Then:

"I didn't expect you," she said rapidly, guiltily, as though we had caught her preening before a mirror. "Not until dinner. I cooked pot roast."

The pot roast was a diversion. She was embarrassed, and she wanted to distract us. Once, more than a decade before, I must have hinted at some huge enthusiasm for pot roast, because, ever since I left for college, my mother has insisted that pot roast is my favorite meal. Letters tempt me home with promises of pot roast. On Thanksgiving a pot roast sits on the platter where a turkey should be. When I arrive for an unexpected visit, my mother links her greeting with an apology if there is no pot roast in the refrigerator.

Because the ritual joined us, I always slipped into my part, rolling my eyes and smacking my lips, burlesquing my approval and hoping that exaggeration masked my indifference.

Before kissing us hello, she removed her glasses as though she were entering familiar territory. Carefully, she folded each earpiece. Carefully, she tucked the glasses into their powder-blue case, which she snapped shut and which she gripped so tightly that her knuckles mottled white and pink. My grandmother, my mother's mother, used to clutch things like that to keep her hands from trembling.

But I can also remember when my grandmother's

hands, like my mother's, could coax cards to defy their fluttering nature. Her back rigid, she would peer over the tops of her glasses at the tower she had built from my grandfather's bridge deck. My children would never see their grandmother that young.

My children. My unborn children. That was another space in my mother's life. Seeing her made me want to give her the gift of grandchildren. The imagined announcement, the reaction, my mother's squinting smile, her cheeks bulging until her eyes were nearly closed, the wave of approval she would radiate—as she had when I first learned how to pick up a spoon or tie my shoes—all that pleased me.

Being with my mother touched into life an efficient deceit. I was tempted to lie, to pat Maxie's belly, and to discuss whether the baby would be a girl or a boy. So much of the love between my mother and me was a con, and much of the con was an effort not to show how afraid we were of each other. Having developed baroque strategies to avoid expressing our real love, we then had to invent even more elaborate tactics to pretend another kind of love we did not feel.

As we kissed hello, my mother groped for my fingers; and we shook hands in solemn formality. Her cheek smelled of cloves and ammonia, whiffs from a sickbed.

"Are you all right?" I asked.

"Yes," she said.

As she got older, she used more make-up, and her face looked flushed beneath the rouge. Her eyes, which had been snapping back and forth among the papers, grayed and watered when she focused on me. After quacking twice to clear her throat, she added:

"I've had the flu ever since your father left." She gazed over my head as she spoke to dismiss both the sickness and my concern. She rarely felt ill; and she didn't want me to think that, alone, she couldn't take care of herself. "Nothing serious."

She was distant with me, as though I were, not a son, but a son-in-law. She embraced Maxie as though she were a blood daughter. Maxie stiffened in my mother's arms. She tucked her chin and arched her back. Having pecked my mother punctiliously on the forehead, a condescending kiss, she retreated to the sofa at the other end of the room. My mother's greetings always embarrassed her with their warmth.

My mother plucked at her skirt as though she were gathering tiny balls of dust. Whenever she was embarrassed, she picked at herself: at the spoon-shaped indentation in her throat, at the bone bump between her breasts where the lowest ribs meet, at her waist, at her hair, pulling out a gray curl, the tip of which she would roll between her thumb and first finger. Every touch reassured her that she was real.

Ever since she was a child, a recurring nightmare in which she gradually dematerialized had tormented her. She would wake mewing; and, before she could go back to sleep, she would climb out of bed and stand before the dresser mirror, touching herself, convincing herself that she was a solid whole being. When she was snubbed or ignored, this same terror of vanishing, of becoming a ghost, seized her.

The first ghost she saw (when she was twelve) was a stranger, a corpulent gentleman in suspenders who surprised her one midnight when she was on her way to the bathroom. He sat at the head of the stairs, his hands folded in his lap, gazing up at a rip in the wallpaper. She assumed he was one of her parents' friends. On the way back to her bedroom, she asked if he was all right and could she get him anything. As she approached, he faded away.

Puzzled, she walked to her bedroom and, turning, glanced back at the top of the stairs. There he was again, sitting in the same position as before, except now he was staring at her. She screamed. A crack of light winked on beneath her parents' closed door; but, when they rushed into the hall, the top step was empty.

My mother's mother died on the Fourth of July, 1960, when she slipped in her dining room doorway and landed flat on her back, still holding the dripping platter above her breast as the roast turkey sailed back over her broken head and, landing on the kitchen floor, slid in its grease under a ladderback chair.

Two years later, my mother, a slave to her compulsions, having padded downstairs at three in the morning to make sure the kitchen faucets were turned off, discovered on the kitchen floor my grandmother's ghost, lying on its back with a startled look in its oval eyes. Fascinated, my mother shuffled toward the ghost, which reached up to her. My mother leaned over. As the transparent fingers touched her palms, her wrists went cold as though she had plunged her hands into an icy stream, and her forearms turned milky, like smoke swirling in glass tubes. In the morning, I found her slumped against the cabinets beneath the sink, one of her fluffy pink slippers leaning on its side under the table, the other dangling from the toes of her left foot.

Because she believed in a spiritual world, my mother clung to the material world. Sensations—the soured-milk smell of the refrigerator, the taste of coffee, the roughness of a washcloth, the band of heat that clamped around her forehead when she peered into the hot oven, the sigh of an aerosol spray, the Africa-shaped stain above the kitchen radiator—were proof against raids from the sinister world of shades, which was eclipsed by the world of the living, but which threatened to erupt in the steam from hot soup or the reflection of a flame on the curved surface of a glass of ginger ale. That other world spoke with the labial sounds of wind in the flue or the hiss of the radio after the station has signed off the air or the bland tone on which a slighting phrase—like Maxie's greeting, "It's good to see you, Mrs. Clay!"—glides.

Grunting, my mother stooped to grab, from the top of a stuffed shoe box, a photograph, which she thrust out before her as though she were warding off a vampire with a cross.

"I've saved this for you," she lied, handing the bribe to Maxie: a pudgy two-year-old in a watery-blue playsuit and a yellow-and-blue-striped jersey sat laughing and rocking in a wooden duck in the dark front hall of my parents' first apartment. I had hated that duck. Seeing the photograph evoked the acrid shellac smell of the rocker. Even the wan colors with which my mother had tinted the picture reminded me of the dismal hours during which I desperately rocked after my mother had strapped me safely into the duck. In it, I could not prevent the thing from rocking. Even when I tried to sit motionless, it rocked. Once, I wailed and bellowed until I was out of breath, unable to believe (with whatever infant judgment I possessed), but beginning to realize that no one would come and rescue me. I think that is my earliest memory. If there is a hell and if I am condemned to it, I have no doubt for my punishment I will be buckled into that duck and set rocking for eternity.

"Remember how much you loved that duck?" my mother said.

"No," I said, hurt although not surprised that my mother's memory denied my own. Didn't she remember how much I had wept? Or was one grim afternoon infecting my memories of dozens of happier ones? The thought that I may have been wrong disturbed me, as though a change in that memory would set off a series of readjustments in all the later memories that rested on it, as though all memory itself were one of my grandmother's fragile card towers.

"We could never get him out," my mother told Maxie. "When the duck finally started falling apart, we had to sneak it out of the house and drive it to the dump after he was asleep."

My mother admitted that deception for my benefit as well as for Maxie's. By taking me into her confidence and explaining how neatly she had fooled me when I was a child, she was trying to build an alliance with the adult me against the child me; but the child lives in the adult, and hearing her confess what I always had known nudged my discomfort into anger.

My childhood had been a sinister time of vanishing objects. Nothing was dependable. Whenever my parents had wanted to get rid of something they thought my sister or I cared about, they waited until after we had gone to bed before smuggling it (a broken but favored tricycle, a television they had decided to return, a cat that refused to be box-trained) away. When I was a child, sleep terrified me, because I never knew what would be gone when I woke.

"You were clever," I said.

"He's in a bad mood," my mother said.

Maxie smiled at the photograph of me in the duck.

"How old were you here?" she asked. "Two? I've never seen a picture of you this young."

I grabbed the photograph from Maxie and tossed it into the fireplace. One corner curled into an acid-green waterdrop-shaped flame. The pale blue playsuit browned. My mother stuck her hand into the fire, yanked out the photograph, waved it until it stopped burning, and dropped it on the slate in front of the fireplace. She put the side of her index finger in her mouth and, from the way her jaw moved up and down, seemed to be chewing away the pain. Without speaking, she left the room.

"What's so important about the picture?" I asked.

When Maxie picked up the photograph, it released a carbon flake, which drifted down to the yellow rug.

"It wasn't yours to throw away," she said.

Maxie and I slept in the attic, which was reserved

for old clothes and guests—a long room with a sloping ceiling. In her general cleaning of the past few days, my mother had unearthed the cardboard cartons that years ago she had buried in the crawl space under the eaves. She had unpacked the boxes and stacked, beneath the guest room's low window, Hannah's childhood scrapbooks (bulging with faded ticket stubs, tarnished silver dollars, a crushed sepia rose that looked like a balled-up Kleenex soaked in dried blood), envelopes stuffed with high school notes, programs from plays I had been in, a collection of brittle, yellowing comic strips I had cut from the Sunday funnies, the remains of my ninth-grade science project on flying saucers . . . On the floor, at the foot of the bed, sprawled an insect-shaped Exercycle, its narrow aluminum tubes poking the air. My father had given it to my mother on her forty-sixth birthday, a gift that had incited her, for the only time in her life, to slap my father's face. To prove he had not meant to insult her, my father puffed away on the machine for fifteen minutes every morning until my mother, afraid he would have a heart attack, forgave him.

Maxie dove into her nightgown and, her face hidden in the cloud of cloth, asked, "If you hate your family so much, why did you want to come?"

Her head poked through the billowing flannel, as though, after having touched on a dare the muddy bottom of a lake and swum back up, she had broken the surface of the water with a gasp.

"They're my parents," I said.

Whenever I struggle free of my family, some love, disguised as a scruple, hooks me, or some gesture I have unwittingly stolen from my parents—the way, after a meal, I clear my throat while putting down my fork; or the way, when nervous, I rub the small of my back with the knuckles of my right hand—startles me. Certain idiosyncracies—the way I push up my glasses, for example, by clasping them between my thumb and third finger—can be traced to my grandparents and perhaps even beyond in a dizzy dance to my great-grandparents and great-great-grandparents and great-great-great-grandparents, all the way back to a hairless primate, squatting on the edge of a grassy plain, who placed his third finger and newly opposable thumb on his temples as he shaded his eyes from the sun's glare.

"We shouldn't have come," I said. "What does she expect me to do? I don't know where my father went."

"She needs you just to be here," said Maxie.

"I feel trapped," I said.

Maxie, her hair falling over her face, crawled across the mattress.

"By your mother?" she asked.

"By families," I said.

Once, at an Israeli cousin's wedding, I had drunkenly joined a chain of dancers and, my arms locked around the shoulders of two stomping uncles, was unable to disengage myself when the heat and the booming music made me nauseated. The enthusiastic groom, one arm free, waved the band on as he led us in a tightening spiral until I was crushed among my sweaty relatives.

When I slipped under the bed sheets, Maxie hooped her arms over my head in a hug and wound her legs through mine.

"Trapped," she said.

"Don't," I said; and, when she wouldn't let go, I reached behind my neck and, grabbing her wrists, broke her hold.

"That hurt," she said, kneeling, holding out her hands as though to show me the pain.

"I'm suffocating," I said. I jumped from the bed and yanked up the window.

When I was a child, after my mother had closed and locked my bedroom windows to protect me from the unseen, I would slip out of my bed, unlock and open the windows to let the unseen in. Something generous about the night and its mysteries delighted me. I would lie on my back, the sensitive spot on the top of my head touching the wall, which served as the bed's headboard; and I would concentrate on the smells and the sounds that drifted in to me: the whiffs of my father's sweet maple tobacco; the creak of the wicker rocker and the regular thump of his feet hitting the floor of the back porch, where he sat in the evening unless driven inside by storms or cold; the slamming of a car door, which if it came late enough, long after most people in our neighborhood were asleep, hinted at the adventures of travel or arrival, both starting points for dreams about my future; the cough of someone out for a walk before bed, an embarrassingly intimate noise; the throbbing of a bass drum, which was the only sound that carried across Forest Park from the old-fashioned bandstand where some band whose origins I never discovered practiced from April to late November. The pulse of that drum, almost felt rather than heard, transformed the night into a dark heart, huge, moved by and moving incomprehensible forces. It was a sexual sound; and its rhythm carried, like a rubber raft on a heaving ocean, my first erotic dreams, fantasies in which ghostly women, whose faces would turn away from me as I woke and tried to possess their images, joined me in empty barns, attic rooms, hidden glades, places that were isolated and therefore enchanted. Halfway through the summer before I entered seventh grade, when I was a moody twelve-year-old determined to rouse mystery at an infuriatingly ordinary camp in West Gloucester, Massachusetts, I saw from my bunkroom window one twilight a girl picking flowers on a finger of land across the river. I ran to the boathouse and illegally—according to camp rules, it was the after-dinner rest hour—took a canoe, which I paddled to the field where the girl had been; but I was unable to find her, and the sense of loss had made me weep. I was convinced that the girl I had seen was the ingenue who in the repertory company of my dreams played, not only various loves, but also the mysterious non-sexed Ariel who, even when I was as young as six, had been wooing me with promises of some extraordinary and never sufficiently explained escape.

This spirit of air was the unseen being for whom I opened my windows. On rare nights, in the moments when sounds cracked open to disclose previously hidden meanings, I could detect the presence of this creature who was squatting on the sill of my consciousness, about to jump down into a dream. Trying not to frighten it away, pretending not to notice it, I would travel, in what was supposed to be an imitation of sleep's nonchalant restlessness, halfway down the bed while rolling from my back to my right side. I would draw up my right leg and stretch my left leg so my toes could slip into the cool long pocket made by the tucked sheet and the bottom edge of the mattress. I would nudge my nose into the crook of my arm to sniff my own odor—which at twenty-six years old I discovered was the smell of raw peanuts. While visiting a friend at a commune in Charlemont, Massachusetts, I found a row of gallon jars and, moving along the counter, sampled the contents of each one: sunflower seeds, organic raisins, toasted soybeans, almonds, walnut halves. When I unscrewed the top of the jar of unroasted peanuts and recognized the familiar smell, I was vexed by the realization that, just as my personality is a patchwork of quirks filched from my ancestors, the physical qualities that make me *me* are mimicked from the material world. That night, after eating supper with the commune, I had walked into the dark field behind their house and discovered the crooked bow of my mouth smiling from a fresh wound in the flank of a fox that, stunned by the beam of my flashlight, froze for a second in the short grass, its small head cocked and one front paw raised.

I have always felt, not trapped by, but tangled in the material world. When I was a child, I was sure the sylph I waited for could rescue me from what seemed an overwhelmingly intricate reality as easily as I might free a moth that had blundered into a spider's web; but it never did, because every night, after I had fallen asleep, my mother, on her way to bed, would stop in my room again to close and lock my windows.

"What is she afraid of?" Maxie asked. She was propped up on her right elbow, her cheek in her hand, a gray-blue vein forking under the tight skin of her wrist.

"Disorder," I said.

"Like you?"

"I don't want to end up muddled like her." I was annoyed by the truth of the comparison. "I don't spend my life collecting my past in cardboard boxes."

"Not in boxes, no," said Maxie. "Don't you feel anything for the things she saved for you?"

"Nothing."

"Don't you want to be able to show your children what you were like before you were their father?"

"I'll be the same," I said, feeling uneasily that I had answered both parts of a two-part question.

"I wish we had more pictures of the way we were," said Maxie, "of the way we are now."

"Why?" I asked. "So thirty years from tonight, when we're unhappy with the way our lives turned out, we can sit around, convincing ourselves things used to be wonderful?"

"If we were happier now, we'd want to have pictures to remind us of what things were like."

"I want to be happy enough when I'm sixty so I don't have to depend on being cheered up by the good old days."

Maxie flopped on her left side, facing away from me.

"I don't want to wait until I'm sixty to be happy," she said.

"Do you want me to buy you a camera tomorrow?" I

asked. The sad and unfamiliar way she had curled up under the sheet disturbed me. She was sinking under my impatience, which, by making me feel cruel, shocked and aroused me. I wanted to pull her from the wall and slap her until she stopped withdrawing and pushed back against me.

"I don't want you to do anything," she said, "except let me sleep."

Left alone, as Maxie retreated into sleep, I poked through the jumble of souvenirs under the windows and picked up *Houdini's Book of Party Magic*, which when I was in the sixth grade had promised a smug power over my friends. For a year I had practiced palming coins, fanning cards, tying knots that vanished when you yanked the string, cracking covered eggs that were whole when the handkerchief was flipped away; but the book's secrets were scientific, not occult. Houdini's magic powder turned out to be baking soda, and water refused to become wine without three drops of food coloring. Nowhere in the index could I find the trick illustrated on the front cover, where a surprised man, wearing a Norfolk jacket and knickers, floated three feet off the floor while Houdini controlled his ascent with a papal gesture.

Tucked inside the cover was a snapshot of five grinning adults, who are lying on their backs in my maternal grandparents' living room. Stepping into the upper left-hand corner of the picture is my grandfather's easy chair, the hem of its slipcover daintily raised, disclosing a mahogany lion's paw. Rising out of the frame is a wing-tipped shoe, its toe pointing at the middle supine figure, my mother. On her right are my aunt Sarah, right arm crooked, holding a cigarette above her cheek, and my mother's cousin Ruth, whose hands, fingertips touching, lie on her humped belly. On the back of the photograph was the penciled date, July '51, two months before Ruth died in childbirth. On my mother's left are two more cousins, Edith (eyes closed, right arm thrown back over her head) and Paula (mouth open, arms rigid at her sides), who were killed with their husbands in 1963, on their way to dinner at the Red Lion Inn in Stockbridge, Massachusetts. Their Lincoln pulled from behind a trailer-truck and slammed into an Oldsmobile going in the opposite direction.

My mother also had saved my Ambassador Photograph Album, which had, embossed on the maroon leatherette cover under the script name, the gilt outline of a figure in top hat and swallowtail coat. On the first black page only two photographs remained tucked into the triangular corner mounts. One was of my maternal grandmother a year before she died. She is sitting in front of a bright kitchen window, the two horns of a straight-backed chair sticking up above her shoulders. Her hands, palms up, are folded in her aproned lap, her mouth is twisted into a tilde-shaped quirky smile, and her right eye—was she winking at the camera?—is closed. The other photo was of my father's father, wearing a bowler far back on his head, his thumbs stuck into the pockets of a checked, half-unbuttoned vest, and of one of his brothers-in-law, my father's uncle Nathan, sleeves rolled up to his biceps, wearing a felt hat that is pulled down so its brim hides his eyes. Nathan developed a palsy a year after he sold his clothing store. He spent the last four months of his life in front of a color television set, one hand trembling on his chair arm, the other hand trembling on the remote-control box in his lap. When his wife found him dead, he was sitting stiffly in his chair, his head thrown back, his eyes wide, his mouth wrenched open as though he were screaming, his fingers clamped down on the remote-control button. On the television screen, a vicious circle of programs and static flashed past: static, western, static, quiz show, jungle movie, static, kiddie show, static, war movie, static, soap opera, static, static . . .

I had lied to Maxie. The things my mother had saved for me did evoke memories, but the images, like the snapshots, were flat. You could not turn them around to see the face of the mysterious woman, climbing out of the Buick in front of which my mother, Hannah, and I are posing. You could not tilt them to see, beyond the edge, the person who is making Hannah laugh so hard she is slipping off the couch. All you could see is the coy way she has thrown her arm across her forehead and how one foot is carefully testing the floor to control her staged tumble. We are all trapped in remembered moments in the same way that, in the photograph I had tried to burn, I am trapped in that rocking duck. I did not want to remember.

I slipped into bed next to Maxie and drifted to sleep, dreaming of the last picture I had looked at in my old photograph album. I have just jumped off the end of a diving board. I am jack-knifing, will continue to jack-knife, forever intolerably suspended six feet above the water.

I am trying to flip over a large turtle, which lies on its back in a dirt road. But the stick I am using bends; and, whenever I lift the turtle on one side, it shifts its weight inside its shell toward me. I don't understand why it wants to remain helpless on its back. Its head is drawn so deeply into its shell that only its open beak is visible. Its warty legs make a futile swimming motion in the air. I wedge my foot under the top shell and lift. There are blackberry brambles behind me. I am afraid of losing my balance and falling into the thorns. The sound of running water comes muted from under the road. I lift my foot once more, trying to heave the turtle over; and I flip myself out of sleep. I became aware almost simultaneously of the camphor smell of the moth-proofed wool blanket that I had dragged up from the foot of the bed where it had been folded, a pressure in my bladder, and a bitter taste that I associate with the smell of the reddish-orange urine a body produces when it is dehydrated. When I opened my eyes, instead of seeing the tops of the rhododendrons outside our bedroom window in Leverett, I was staring at dirty green wallpaper with a repetitious jungle design out of which, every nine inches, the same tiger stared back at me from behind the same clump of bushes.

I was lying on my back, my right hand resting on my sticky chest, my left hand tucked between Maxie's thighs. Nine years ago, when I first fumbled Maxie in the field behind the summer stock theater where we were both apprenticed, she had interrupted my groping to tell me that I was the first beau to touch her crotch before touching her breasts. Her right leg was flung across my left ankle. When I slipped free, she chewed on some rubber word, rolled onto her belly, and crawled crabwise away from me to her edge of the bed.

As I climbed to the floor, a spring twanged like a frog.

"Yump," answered Maxie, who commands an extensive and complex sleep language. During the first year we lived together, I tried to break the code of her mutterings, partly for the power of knowing her dreamy secrets, but more for the chance to master the mysterious vocabulary of the unconscious, which with its grunts and snorts complements in a paleolithic way the ghostly cave drawings that decorate the inside of a sleeping skull. But there were few repetitions. Her random bursts, clickings, and hisses reminded me more of faulty plumbing than occult speech—sounds you might hear in an ancient apartment building: on the third floor, the old lady with the red birthmark on her cheek just flushed the toilet; on the ninth floor, the couple with the cats are running the tub taps.

My mother also talks in her sleep, not with Maxie's clear percussions (cymbals, xylophone, brushes on the snare drum), but with fading woodwinds, mournful glissandos that slip up the scale into either silence or a sound beyond the reach of the listening ear. When I used to return from school to find my mother napping on the living room couch, I would sit across from her, a book open in my lap (in case she woke suddenly), rapt, waiting for her to betray some part of the lore that I assumed all adults used to survive in the world's common confusion.

My wife and my mother share other habits. Both suffer guilt when buying clothes for themselves. As a result, both return from shopping trips laden with gifts for others. They have poor memories. Maxie loses wallets and leaves keys in the ignition when she locks the car. My mother, one forgotten cigarette poking over the edge of the kitchen table, another balanced on the cap of a ketchup bottle, can light a third that will burn itself out in a living room ashtray, a fourth that she will abandon in an empty tuna fish can (found in the backyard, picked up to throw away, and left on the back porch), a fifth that she will lay on a saucer and that she will find hours later stuck with dried coffee to the china. Both bump, bruise, and burn themselves a dozen times a day. Like the plastic models of women whose insides are visible, their bodies are, for them, receptacles to be packed with experience rather than points of reference in a process. Neither of them can read road maps. When I am driving and Maxie hesitantly navigates, I attack her with the same sarcasms my father uses on my mother when they are in a car. I have seen each woman, while describing a place on Cape Cod, crook an arm over her head like a ballet dancer in fifth position, making of her flesh a map that is as puzzling as any picked up in a gas station. Bourne nestles under the armpit, Chatham pokes out at the elbow, Race Point hangs from the tip of the index finger, and Long Point curls around with the thumb. Maxie, harder, more secure, makes a rigid map; my mother's map is limp.

"She's like your cousin Elaine," my mother says when describing Maxie to relatives, "except more flat-chested," seeing in Maxie's meager breast a lack of warmth, which she attributes to all non-Jews.

As I walked downstairs from the attic to the second floor, the carpet runner, which my father for a decade had been promising to retack, slipped and bulged under my bare feet. The cool air stripped me of a drowsy security and made my nakedness vulnerable. Blinded by the dark, I toddled with increasing slowness toward the bathroom, arms extended and hands groping for the doorknob, until my toes touched the glassy beginning of a tiled floor and I realized that I had walked through what had seemed to be the solid wood of the bathroom door. With rocking robot-like steps, all lift in the hips, legs stiff, preparing for contact with something hard, I half turned, stopping when my right knee hit the front of the toilet bowl. Like an old man, bracing himself for balance, I reached down and found the cool enamel tank top, before swinging around to sit. Elbows on knees, hands propping my forehead, I closed my eyes, imagining the dark vacancy between my feet where the familiar star-shaped system of cracks in the tile should have been. I lulled myself into a languor with a crepitation that sounded like a death rattle followed by the sigh of an escaping soul and the hiss of my urine against the inside slope of the toilet bowl, a liquid sound that was joined by a subtle sloshing from the direction of the tub. Standing, I swung my arm over my head until the light cord brushed against my wrist. I pulled the string, blinked in the bright whiteness of the bathroom at my mother, who, stretched out in a tubfull of gray water, blinked back. As she pushed herself up into a sitting position, her freckled tubular breasts, floating in the water, flopped against her chest. Water spilled along the creases between her waist and thighs as though she were inflating like the rubber women advertised in the back pages of men's magazines. Her eyes, in the glare, were black sockets. I pulled the string, snapping off the light.

"Sorry," I said.

The afterimage of the tessellated floor became, as it faded, a net into which I had stepped, a web in the center of which my mother waited.

"What are you doing?" I asked. "It's the middle of the night."

"I couldn't sleep," she said; and then, instead of retreating before my anger, partly from embarrassment, partly to make amends, she started explaining in her slurred slow voice what had kept her awake:

"Your father's not the only one who can leave. I'm going away too. I'm going to sell the house and go around the world. I was going to when I got out of college. I thought if I could just get away from everything I knew, go somewhere no one knew me, I could . . . I don't know, do something important. But you were born. Hannah was born. I've never had a chance to be free. I always had to be worrying about someone else."

"That's an excuse," I said.

"It's not an excuse," she said. "It's not. I cared about you. I wanted you to have nice clothes, toys, what you wanted, what you needed."

The water sloshed as she changed position in the tub.

I said, "Mom," which sounded foreign, the way words do after you have repeated them too often.

She did not answer. I stood in the doorway and said, "Good night."

"Dennis," my mother said, "that was the first time I've seen you naked since you were a little boy."

To dodge my embarrassment, I said, "You should leave. You should free yourself," realizing what I meant was: go, free me.

When Maxie and I came downstairs for breakfast the next morning, my mother, dressed in a white sleeveless blouse that had her initials embroidered in white thread on the bosom, was holding the map of France to the front hall wall with her forearm, while she pried loose a tack with a butter knife.

"I'm not going," she said. "I got a letter from your father this morning, Dennis. He's gone to New York to meet your grandfather. After avoiding him for twenty-two years, suddenly he's decided he's got to talk to him." She took down the map, angrily snapped it along its creases, folded it, and packed it in a cardboard box along with the pictures of Paris, the Loire, and the Riviera. "I want you to bring your father home."

Four

The only time I met my father's father was on a trip to Providence, Rhode Island, in the fall of 1949. I was eight. To celebrate our visit, my grandmother planned to butcher a chicken. My mother, afraid the slaughter would terrify me, sent me from the kitchen.

Having recently read the story of Abraham and Isaac in a Saturday morning Bible class, I conjured up an exotic murder to fit the noises that I heard behind the shut door—flutterings, wing-whirrings, shouts, the crash of glass (while swinging the bird over her head to break its neck, my grandmother slammed a pitcher from a shelf).

"What's that?" asked my father as he wiped his glasses on a crocheted antimacassar.

"She's got a live chicken in there," I said.

Hannah ran to peek. She returned, reaching up behind her head to unsnap her terrier-shaped barrette, and said, "I'm not going to eat that."

There was a hideous scream in the kitchen. Hannah and I both looked at my father, who had plunged into a Russian grammar book he had brought and now sat, staring at the piano, making the alien sounds of soft *l*'s and palatal *r*'s. I sneaked across the dining room and, opening the door a crack, peered into the kitchen.

My mother was kneeling under the window, sweeping glass shards into a dustpan, her back to me. My grandmother, her hair wrapped in a turquoise babushka, humming Brahms' "Lullaby," stood at the table, smoothing the dead chicken's feathers.

I wandered back to the living room and, having tucked myself into a corner of the sofa, picked up the Providence *Journal*'s Sunday comic supplement, in which I discovered "The Little King," "The Katzenjammer Kids," and "Henry." Our Springfield *Republican* comics, which offered the denser adult worlds of "Terry and the Pirates," "Steve Canyon," and "Dick Tracy," seemed by comparison gloomy.

My father, pausing between Lesson Three and Lesson Four, asked, "Did I tell you about the time my father went after me with a butcher knife?"

"I don't think I want to meet him," said Hannah.

When he arrived in a taxi, we gathered on the front porch to greet him. Ponderously, moving his buttocks in a semicircle, he backed from the cab. Facing away from us, he straightened up, tugged at the flukes of his tuxedo jacket, and, spreading his arms, he turned in place.

"Moses!" he cried, "Ethel!" He lumbered across the walk and stomped up the steps, his arms still spread, as though he were playing airplane.

"Aaron," said my grandmother, "what have you done?"

"I rented them yesterday," my grandfather said, "and kept them at the store. How do I look?"

He was splendid, ragged up in tails and top hat, swinging a glass-knobbed cane, the tip of which he tapped on each of my shoulders when we were introduced. He wore spats and shiny pinstriped pants. His waxed mustaches curled around at the ends into parentheses that enclosed a dimpled upper lip. Bushy black eyebrows hung in Babylonian splendor over his eyelids. His white hair was combed back into a ducktail, although because he was fifty-seven the style was more distinguished than rowdy.

The five of us milled on the porch as he invented a courtesy for each. He kissed Hannah's hand. Her eyes widened; and, furtively, she clasped the spot his lips had touched. With a flourish, he bowed to my mother, who scowled over his bent head. He shook both my father's hands, folding them together between his big palms. Before his wife, he paused.

"Pauline," he said, repeatedly nodding, "I told you they'd finally come."

My grandfather grew up in Plissa, Vilna Gubernia. His father managed an estate for a count. The word conjured up capes, Transylvanian drawls, a world where wolves walked on hind legs and bowed when they met you in the forest.

"Did you ever see a wolf?" I asked.

"One evening," said my grandfather, hunching toward me from where he sat at the foot of the bed, "as I was going home through the woods, I saw a wolf walking beside the path. I walked faster, but it walked faster too. When I started to run, it ran, turning its head to look at me. It kept me company all the way home.

And, if you had to go outside at night, you could see the eyes of the wolves sitting around the house in the dark." He grabbed my left ankle through the blanket. I jumped.

"It was cold there," he said. "On Passover, the river would still be frozen. When we'd walk across the ice, the cracks underneath the surface would explode. Awful. Sometimes I'd wake up in the middle of the night and listen to the rumble caused by a split in the ice that would start a mile away and roar along the river like a train."

My grandfather's favorite story, however, did not take place at night. After slipping an opal from his trouser pocket, he described the brass chest that the count had given his father and that his father had given him. It had been filled with semiprecious stones.

"This is all that's left," he said, handing me the opal. "I've kept it with me ever since I left Plissa forty-one years ago."

My sister leaned across the space between our beds and took the stone.

"Who will you give it to when you die?" she asked.

"Young lady," he said, "don't talk to me about dying." He held out his hand, and Hannah slapped the stone into his palm. Sticking out his right leg and rolling slightly to the left, he shoved the memento back into his pocket.

"The chest had a lock made of bone," he said. "I used to carry its key on a string around my neck; and one day, when I was walking in the fields, a girl grabbed it and stuck it down here," he gestured to the V made by his open shirt collar. "Well, I went after it, and it was so pleasant in there I forgot all about the key."

Throwing back his head, he roared.

"I forgot," he gasped, his face blotching red, "all about the key."

My grandmother, who also had grown up in Plissa, stopped in the bedroom doorway. Folding a checkered bath towel, she said, "What I remember about you was when I came by your house and saw you standing in the middle of the room, carrying your dead brother, Saul, in your arms. You looked so surprised. Saul died of smallpox," she explained, "and Aaron just stood there, holding him and looking puzzled."

When he was sixteen, my grandfather walked from Plissa to Berlin, where upon arriving he asked directions to a particular address.

"The man said, 'Run down this street and run up that street,'" my grandfather said. "In German the word meant *walk*, but in Yiddish it meant *run*. So I followed his directions and ran even though it seemed pretty strange."

"The best thing," my grandmother interrupted, "was when you first came to America. You and Frank took dancing lessons."

My grandfather, prepared for the story, winked at me, forming a conspiracy, as though only the two of us could appreciate the anecdote.

"There they were," my grandmother continued, "him," she pointed at my grandfather, "six foot three, and my brother Frank, four foot four, hanging on to each other and waltzing, waltzing together whenever they had the chance. They were so afraid of letting their bodies touch, they held each other out like this." She stuck her arms out straight, as though she were warding off, not dancing with, someone. "I used to laugh so hard."

Hannah, excluded by my grandfather's wink, laughed loudly to prove she understood the joke.

"But, Pauline," said my grandfather, gently suggesting that my grandmother had missed the point of her own tale, "I was a good dancer. That's why you married me."

"That's why Esther married you," said my grandmother.

Esther Chodis, my grandfather's first wife, my father's mother, had grown up in a village near Plissa, but she did not meet Pauline and become her friend until they both came to America.

"She was the beauty," said my grandmother, "I was the brains. When she found out that Aaron liked Zola, she had me read *Germinal* and tell her the plot, so she could impress him. When we lived in New York, we were roommates, and I had to console her over her love affair with Aaron."

"I was a gentleman," said my grandfather.

Gallantly, he wooed and won his cunning Esther by three-stepping into her cagey heart.

"She wanted me to sell dresses," said my grandfather, who in 1911, when he was not selling groceries from a pushcart, slouched around Manhattan looking for a job as a journalist on an American newspaper. He had learned English by struggling through *Leather-Stocking Tales* and a carton of brittle, yellowed copies of Ned Buntline that he found abandoned in their apartment closet the day they moved in. At night, Esther sewed sample dresses for a designer named William Punch, while my grandfather paced through the two rooms, bellowing out passages about Wild Bill Hickock or Wyatt Earp.

"I wanted to go to San Francisco and Denver," said my grandfather, "she wanted to go to Paris."

Through a friend who worked on the sports section of *The Evening Post*, my grandfather met William Barclay Masterson. They got drunk at a sportswriters' bar on Tenth Street and waffled on until three in the morning about Indians, street brawls, gunfights, and boxing.

"Mostly about boxing," said my grandfather, "but other things too. You know, once when he was lost in the desert, my friend Bat Masterson had to drink his own blood to survive. He dared me to do the same. He had a silver knife with his initials on it, and he said he'd give it to me if I'd open a vein and drink my own blood." He rolled back his sleeve and showed me a white crescent on his forearm. He said, "The son-of-a-bitch didn't let me keep the knife."

Mr. Punch, Esther's boss, offered to take her with him to Europe. Tempted, but demure, she said, "Not without my husband"—but she smiled ambiguously. Mr. Punch offered my grandfather a chance to revisit his family in Plissa.

They packed, sent their children—my father and his brother—to Pauline, who had moved to Providence, and sailed in the fall of 1919. My grandfather, after an angry week in Paris, left Esther to her nimble fancy, which bopped back and forth between her husband and her employer.

He arrived in Providence denouncing marriage, swaggeringly defending a new order in which both sex and politics were free of ethical subtlety. Pauline warily agreed that marriages might founder and, since she already had his two children, let him move in. Within a year, they married.

Unwilling to borrow for survival (he would take loans for higher purposes), he sent my father and my uncle to the Mount Sinai Orphanage in Boston, moved with Pauline into a one-room apartment, and began to plot. In 1921, determined to make a fortune in bootleg liquor, he abandoned his grocery pushcart; but his inspired flimflammery was no match for the grim organization of the mobs, so he yielded up both his dreams of an eighty-six proof bonanza and his independence and went to work as a driver for some local racketeers. On a fall day in 1922 he left a warehouse in a truck carrying $30,000 worth of booze, which never reached its assigned destination.

Giddy with what he saw as extravagant opportunity, he drove to New York and sold the stuff on his own. After ditching the truck in Brooklyn, he sent a check for $15,000 to Pauline and advised her not to touch the money for five years and then to buy a house, which she did. Pocketing the other half of his sudden wealth, he fled to France, praying that the gangsters would hunt him there—he had left a message telling them where he was going—rather than in Pauline's apartment.

Hoods questioned and watched her. She vilified my grandfather and slammed into a cozy job, cooking for Jonathan Arthur Brodkin, professor of classics at Brown University. He wanted sirloin; she cooked him gefilte fish. The crooks grudgingly decided she was clean and, after half a year, determined to follow up the lead that they did not believe in.

Paul Morello, a nineteen-year-old gunman from Cranston, Rhode Island, arrived in Paris with a weak will to kill and a fascination with college-bred bohemian girls. He was tall and thin and had a bad complexion.

"He used make-up to cover the pockmarks," said my grandfather, "so his face was as pink as an eraser. Everytime he blew his nose, he wiped off some make-up. By the end of the day, his face still was colored pink, but his nose was white."

Morello only half-heartedly searched for my grandfather. He spent most of his time sitting in cafés, trying to start conversations with American women who, he thought, had come to Paris for romance. He wore a shiny sharkskin suit and shirts with detachable collars. By the time he found my grandfather, he had lost one of his studs. Unable to say anything not included in his French phrase book, he had been too intimidated to go into a store and buy a new stud, so he fastened his shirt and collar with a piece of string.

My grandfather had grown a goatee and was supporting an anarchist art theater that specialized in seminude performances of plays in which Time, Death, and Everyman strode around the stage, declaiming in Shakespearian asides. He lived on a houseboat moored to the Quai Anatole France. The afternoon Morello carefully climbed onto the deck, my grandfather was cooking mussels.

Morello held a gun to my grandfather's temple and explained who he was and why he was there. My grandfather offered to give back what was left of the money. Morello asked where my grandfather kept his clothes. My grandfather opened a cupboard over a bunk, and Morello, the gun still aimed at my grandfather, pointed out a pair of slacks, a turtleneck sweater, and a pair of socks. He was convinced he was having bad luck with women because he was not appropriately dressed; he looked out of place. He had my grandfather roll the clothes into a bundle. Then they sat at the table, across from each other. Morello rested his hand on the tabletop with the gun pointing at my grandfather's chest.

"How do you get the girls to take off their clothes on stage?" asked Morello. "They're too classy to be strippers."

"You've been following me," said my grandfather.

"I could have killed you a week ago," said Morello.

"Can you imagine what that feels like?" my grandfather asked me. "Finding out someone's been following you for a week, trying to decide whether or not to kill you?"

"Why didn't you jump him?" asked my father, who had joined my grandmother in the doorway.

"I did," said my grandfather, answering my father, but looking at me. "I grabbed the gun just like this."

He caught my hand and squeezed it.

"He struggled just like you're doing now," my grandfather said to me.

"You're hurting him," said my father.

"He has a gun," said my grandfather. "Don't you?" he asked me.

I was delighted to be included in my grandfather's story, but I felt uncomfortable in the role he had assigned me. I didn't want to be my grandfather's killer. I wanted to be my grandfather.

My grandfather, having loosened his hold, patted the back of my hand.

"He's been stalking me through the streets of Paris, aiming his gun at me . . . Here," he said, uncurling my index finger and pulling back my thumb, "aim your gun at me. Slowly, he squeezes the trigger. Squeeze the trigger. Not too much. Not enough to shoot. Every time he's about to kill me, he hesitates. Why? Why doesn't he shoot? What kind of a killer are you?" he suddenly shouted at me. "You're not doing your job."

Still pointing my finger at him, ready to shoot with my imaginary gun if I had to, I said, "But you said he didn't."

I was confused. I couldn't tell if I was being dismissed because I had played my role too well or not well enough. If I was Morello, I couldn't shoot my grandfather. But, if I didn't shoot him, I wasn't a good enough gunman to keep my part.

"I'll just have to find someone else to kill me," said my grandfather.

"Me," shouted Hannah, bouncing in her bed. "I'll kill you, I promise."

"That's terrible, Hannah," said my mother, who came up behind my father in the doorway. "Aaron, what are you teaching them?"

"My life," said my grandfather. "I'm telling them the story of my life." My grandfather turned to me and said, "Give your sister the gun. Come on, Dennis. You've had your chance."

Hannah swiped at my hand and came away with her index finger pointed and her thumb cocked.

"Ready," she announced. And then, looking at my hand, which still was pointing an imaginary gun, she said, "That's not fair. You've got to put your finger down. Make him put his finger down."

My grandfather folded back my finger.

"But you jumped him and took the gun away in the boat," I said.

"That's right," said my grandfather.

He held out his hand. Hannah gave him the imaginary gun.

"And you shot him?" I asked, hoping my grandfather would shoot Hannah.

"No," said my grandfather. "I invited him for lunch."

Hannah and I both complained.

"But I did," said my grandfather. "That's what really happened."

Hannah squirreled herself back under her blanket. I plumped up my pillow. My grandfather, realizing he was losing his audience, said, "If I don't have him for lunch, what will I do with all the mussels I'm cooking?"

"Throw them overboard," said Hannah.

My grandfather put his hands on his knees and solemnly asked:

"Even if it's not true?"

Hannah and I exchanged looks and nodded together.

"I threw the mussels overboard," said my grandfather, "and I offered to arm-wrestle him for the money that was left."

"Really?" asked my mother.

My grandfather raised one eyebrow at Hannah and me.

"Really?" he asked us.

"Really," we said.

"We locked fists," said my grandfather. "Which one of you is Morello?"

"I am," said Hannah.

"I was first," I said.

"Both of you arm-wrestle with me," he said.

He leaned over until he was almost lying down. Then, with a startling, agile movement, he flipped around so that, instead of sitting on the edge of the bed, he was kneeling, ready to arm-wrestle. Hannah scooted from her bed to mine. Together, we grabbed my grandfather's raised right hand.

"We locked fists," my grandfather repeated, "and struggled." As he described what had happened, he pushed and pulled our hands, so that first his knuckles and then ours grazed the mattress. "He was very strong. He almost had me down for the count. I thought of the theater I was supporting, the houseboat, the lunch I had thrown overboard, and with a supreme effort, grunting and straining, I finally, almost failing, at last succeeding, pinned his hand down on the table, and won. "

Hannah and I pulled our hands away.

"I told him he could keep the clothes he had stolen from me," said my grandfather, "and I offered to get him some twine to tie them up. Before we arm-wrestled I had put the gun on the floor. While I rummaged in a locker for twine, he picked up the gun."

"Did he shoot you?" Hannah asked.

"I ran away," he said. "Wouldn't you?"

"No," I said.

"What would you have done?" he asked me.

"Shoot," I said.

"I didn't have the gun," he said.

"You had it before," I said.

"Do I look like I could murder somebody?" my grandfather asked me. "Don't turn your head. Look at me. Do you think this is all a joke?"

"Where'd you run to?" my father asked, trying to save me from my grandfather's anger.

"He thinks I could *murder*." He stretched out the word as though he enjoyed saying it.

He folded his arms over his chest and pouted like a child.

"He thinks you're a hero," said my mother.

Looking sideways at me, he asked, "Do you?"

I nodded.

He grinned.

"He's not, Dennis," my mother said. "He did stupid things."

"Where'd you run to?" my father asked again.

"You don't like me," my grandfather said to my mother.

"I don't respect you," she told him .

"Do you like me?" he insisted.

Trying to resist a smile, my mother said, "I like you."

My grandfather heaved himself up and waddled across the room. My grandmother and father stepped aside. Grabbing my mother in a hug, he lifted her off the floor and kissed her, his lips smacking as sharply as a gunshot, on her forehead. A shoe dropped from one of her dangling feet. When he put her down, she straightened her dress and said, "You're just like Moses. You'd rather be liked than respected."

"And you?" asked my grandfather.

"I want to be respected," she said. "Finish your story. It's getting late."

My grandfather stared at my mother until she looked at the floor, bent over, and put her shoe back on. Walking to the bed, he said, "There's not much else to tell."

Kneeling up on the mattress, I shouted at my mother, "You're ruining everything."

Turning to my father, she asked, "What am I ruining?"

"There was a mood," said my father.

My mother dug at the cuticle of her thumb with the nail of her index finger, which made a ticking sound, as though she were a bomb about to explode. She licked her lips, as she always does when she is upset, a childish gesture. When she spoke, she whined. She never gets angry like an adult.

"Everyone else can come in and listen except me," she said.

"You're judging him," said my father.

"You're not?" she asked. "What did you say on the way here? Tell him what you said."

"I don't want to know," said my grandfather.

My mother started, "He said you—"

"I don't want to know," my grandfather shouted.

Quickly and at the same time, as though choreographed, my father put his arm around my mother's shoulders to comfort and restrain her, my grandmother touched my mother's cheek with the tips of her fingers, and my grandfather clapped his hands over his ears.

My mother shook herself free.

"I don't want to ruin anything," she said.

My grandfather took his hands away from his ears and hesitantly held them chest high like a begging dog.

"Do you want to finish the story?" asked my father.

When my grandfather didn't answer, my mother said, "I want to hear what happened."

Talking quickly and in a monotone, my grandfather said, "I had some money in my pocket. I got on a train. I decided to ride until I came to somewhere beautiful."

He got off the train in a Swiss village called Château d'Oex. As he described the place, he began to speak more slowly, his tone rising and falling for emphasis, as though the contours in his voice could create for us the hills and valleys of the town.

It was the end of September. The cows were being

driven down from the upland pastures. Each one wore a different size bell, and all the bells clanged as the cows swung their heads. They wandered from my grandfather's story through my imagination, smelling of heated hide, hay, and souring milk. Slobber drooled from their mouths. Their lower jaws moved in circles as they chewed. They blinked their eyes and twitched their ears at the flies.

The men driving the cows wore gray lederhosen. Some of the girls wore white blouses with short sleeves as fluffly as whipped cream and dirndls of a blue so dark the pattern looked like flowers scattered on oil.

"It was like walking into a fairy tale," said my grandfather.

Conspiratorially, he whispered to Hannah and me, "Close your eyes and picture it. The town was surrounded by mountains. In one direction, in the shadows, the mountains were as purple as the plums you had for dessert tonight. In the other direction, in the sunlight, they were green and red and yellow. You could hike up until you reached the snow line. If you stood in one spot, it would be drizzling. If you walked a step or two higher, it would be snowing."

He described the big, gnarled, snakelike tree roots, which I imagined looking like the carved lion's paw legs on the big couch in my grandfather's living room. And he described walking up the spiral path on the small hill in town to the church at the top, which in my mind became a magical trudge toward a castle holding some Goldilocks or Rapunzel captive.

One day, as he was hiking in a meadow on the slopes above the village, he came to a farm. Rather than go around it, he climbed over a fence and started across a pen, when a huge sow, as big as a Saint Bernard and grunting in a most horrible way, charged him. My grandfather vaulted over the nearest fence and met the farmer, who had come around the barn to see what the commotion was about.

The farmer's name was Jacob Spink. He was seventy-three years old. His forehead was webbed with threadlike veins that looked like cracks in an old enamel plate. His beard was the yellow of stained piano keys. And his eyes were so hidden beneath folds of droopy skin they looked like thumb pokes in uncooked bread dough. My grandfather molded the air as he spoke.

Spink's German dialect was close enough to my grandfather's Yiddish for them to communicate. He asked my grandfather what he wanted. My grandfather explained he was lost. Spink, with an Old Testament imagination to match his patriarch's appearance, took my grandfather's words, not geographically, but spiritually. Spink told my grandfather he would help him find his way again.

Leading my grandfather across the barnyard, Spink said God had surely brought my grandfather to the farm. The house was an odd squat building made of logs. From the outside, the walls looked three feet high, as though gnomes lived there, my grandfather said. When the door opened, you stepped down as though you were entering a cellar. The house, built half in a hole so the floor would be below the frost line and stay relatively warm all winter, fitted like a peg into the earth. In the house were four separate apartments, each one chambered like a heart with four rooms.

Two of the apartments were entered from the barnyard. Two, around back, were entered from an herb garden. There was no decoration in any of the rooms and only the most basic furniture. Spink was an Anabaptist. He and the families of his children were living as the Apostles had lived, communally. They shared what they had with each other and with the other Anabaptists who lived not far away on the slopes.

"We have no possessions," Spink said. "What's ours is God's and also yours."

He gave my grandfather apple beer, cold leftover duck, a pudding called *Schuten Krafen* (which was made from flavored cream, curds, bread crumbs, sugar, eggs, and fried onions), a mild yellow cheese, a watery white goat cheese (which my grandfather said tasted like a wet diaper), and a sausage (which was the russet of dried blood and was so greasy it squished as he cut it and left droplets of cloudy white coagulating fat on the knife blade).

"You will stay with us," he told my grandfather.

Over the years, two sons and a son-in-law had died, all of them leaving widows and children. Spink, his daughter, daughters-in-law, and grandchildren cultivated fields held in common with their neighbors, but they needed another man to help at home. Because he had spent most of his money and because their life seemed peaceful, my grandfather stayed for a year and a half, sleeping at first in the barn on a mat of sweet-smelling, prickly, tickling straw. "Every night before I lay down," said my grandfather, "I had to shake the straw to scare out the mice."

Later, once the Anabaptists had grown used to him, he slept inside the house in an attic loft beside a small window through which he could see fields and slopes, pocked and distorted by the bubbles and ripples in the glass.

"When I moved my head," said my grandfather, "the mountains waved."

Years after my grandfather told the story, I realized that whenever I pictured him sleeping in the loft or the barn, vaulting over the pigpen fence, or hiking up the mountainside, I imagined him as he was that fall evening in 1949, a fat old man who grunted when he stood and sighed when he sat. How could he ever have been young?

He fell in love with Spink's granddaughter. (Spink's daughter, my mother claimed, when we reminisced the night before I left for New York to find my father.) Her name was Elizabeth Tschetter. She was, according to my grandfather, plain. Her features were younger, firmer versions of Spink's, and variations on those of her other relatives on their farm and in the surrounding countryside. There had been so much intermarriage among the few Anabaptists left in these mountains that faces shared characteristics, as though they drew their eyes, noses, ears, and mouths (the same way they drew their supplies) from a common storehouse.

"Sitting in a room with my Spinks and Tschetters and the Spinks and Tschetters from other nearby farms," my grandfather said, "was like going to a Hallowe'en party where everyone, but me, wore the same mask."

Elizabeth was not ardent. She was simple and religious. When she talked, she talked directly to the point. When she did chores, she did them efficiently without fuss. She never worried. She envied no one. When she walked, she strode like a man. In a chair, she never slouched, but sat upright, as though her conscience were a plumb-bob that kept her body and soul level.

"She was the happiest person I ever met," my grandfather said. "When I was with her, she made me happy."

In the spring, he asked her to marry him.

"But you were already married," said Hannah.

"Twice," said my grandmother, "and not even one divorce."

"Esther had abandoned me," my grandfather said to my grandmother, "and you . . ."

"Yes?" my grandmother asked.

"You were in Providence, Rhode Island," said my grandfather.

"Before he could marry her," my grandmother said, "he had to get baptised."

"But you're Jewish," said my mother, who gave both Hannah and me a quick explanation of what baptism meant.

"I was born a Jew," said my grandfather. "I am an atheist."

"In any case," said my father, "you're not an Anabaptist."

"I'm sure God didn't mind," said my grandfather, joking.

"How do you know?" I asked, taking him seriously.

My grandfather, after glancing at my father, asked me, "Has your father told you there's a God?"

"No," I said.

"How do you know there is one?" he asked.

I shrugged.

"Let him believe," said my father. And then, retreating, trying to avoid a fight, he added, "It doesn't matter."

"Is there a God?" I demanded.

"Ask your father," said my grandfather.

Typically, my father did not answer my question; he tried to find out the answer I wanted. Instead of telling me what he believed, he asked, "Do you want to believe in God?"

I didn't know if I wanted to believe or not.

"Tell me," I said.

"I can't," said my father.

"Is there?" I asked my grandfather.

"Don't look at me," my father said to my grandfather. "He's asking you."

"There isn't," said my grandfather.

"He gives better answers than I do, doesn't he?" my father said to me.

When I reminded my mother of this incident that night in Springfield before I left for New York, she said, "He answered because he didn't care as much as your father."

"No," said Maxie, who had been sitting quietly listening to my mother and me swap memories, "because he cared more."

My grandfather was baptised on Palm Sunday.

"Did you marry Elizabeth Whatsername?" asked Hannah.

"He did," said my grandmother, "and left her. And she probably never married again since I'm sure she believed in marriage more than he did."

"Did you have any children with her?" my father asked.

"If we did, I would have done what you just did," said my grandfather. "I never would have told them there is no God."

He must have meant his words to be an apology to my father for meddling, but it sounded as if he were rebuking both my father and himself.

"I don't know if she had a child," my grandfather said after a pause. "I hope she did. They needed help on that farm."

"Then why didn't you stay, Aaron?" asked my grandmother.

"I wanted to come home," he said. "But I've never been as happy as I was there."

He left Switzerland and, as he had years before when he left Plissa, walked across Europe, begging. In a restaurant in Le Havre, he saw a man slip a wallet into his coat pocket and drape the coat over a suitcase.

"I bent down and pretended to tie my shoe," said my grandfather. "It was easy to reach into the coat and grab the wallet. I went outside and opened it. He was carrying a lot of money, which I stuffed into my underpants. I was afraid someone would rob *me*, you see. I also found a piece of paper with a woman's name and a telephone number. I think it was a London—or at least an English—telephone number. Long after the stealing stopped bothering me, I used to feel bad, thinking that he was never able to get in touch with that woman."

"You stole?" I asked.

"Haven't you ever stolen anything?" my grandfather asked back sharply. "I'm sure you have."

My father put his hands in his pockets and, waiting for my answer, nervously jingled his keys like a jailer.

"Yes," I said.

"When?" asked my father.

"Last week," I said.

"What?" asked my father.

"A dime," I said.

"Why?" asked my father.

"For a comic," I said.

"Have you done it before?" asked my father.

I nodded.

"Who from?" asked my father.

"You," I said.

"You could have come to me," said my father. "Have I ever said you couldn't have a comic?"

I shook my head no.

"Haven't you ever stolen?" my grandfather, defending me, asked my father.

"When I was poor," said my father. "I needed to survive."

"So did I," said my grandfather.

"He didn't need a comic to survive," said my father, pointing at me.

"No," said my grandfather. "He's different from you and me. He'll never be like us."

"I want to be like you," I said to my grandfather.

"Don't you want to be like your father?" my grandfather asked me.

"I want to go on a farm," I said.

"And meet gangsters?" asked my grandfather. "And cowboys? And pirates?"

"Do you know pirates?" I asked him.

"He's teasing you," said my father. "It's time to go to bed."

"Finish the story," said Hannah.

"It won't be finished till tomorrow," said my grandfather, "and the day after tomorrow and the day after that."

"If you don't finish," my father said, "they won't go to sleep."

"I stole enough money . . ." said my grandfather. He paused and waited for a reaction. When none came, he continued, "to go to England where I became an entrepreneur."

When pressed, he admitted he was a stagehand during bad times.

"Times," he added, "were often bad."

At the Strutters' Club near Picadilly Circus, he played records for strippers—who would not have struck Morello as being too classy to undress on stage. The dark narrow room was decorated with a Confederate flag, and painted on the salmon-colored walls were cartoons of happy blacks cakewalking through the streets of a New Orleans that existed only in the imagination of the club's owner, an old man named Partridge.

"His breath always smelled of chocolate," said my grandfather. "And his skin was as cold as dry ice. His face was horrible, puffy and white, "—my grandfather screwed up his own face as he talked, curling out his upper lip until it almost touched his nose—"and his eyes were small and green." I pictured two peas pushed into a lumpy mound of mashed potatoes.

Partridge sat in the doorway, collecting money from the customers, who, even though they had plenty of headroom, ducked as they entered. A stage ran across the back of the club.

"On each side," my grandfather said, "were heavy purple curtains that were filthy where they dragged on the floor. In the room were maybe a dozen and a half chairs. One man came every evening, sat in the front row with his back to the girls, and read his newspaper in the light from the stage."

Most of the girls were West Indians. They posed naked in *tableaux vivants* or danced to the music. Fats Waller. Count Basie. One girl liked stripping to a Bessie Smith record, "I'm Wild About That Thing."

My grandfather undulated about the room as he told the story, grinding at my father, bumping at my grandmother, who placidly said, "Aaron, remember the children."

The record had a crack halfway through the song. My grandfather, imitating Bessie Smith, sang, with more gargle than gravel, "You press my button, I'm—I'm—I'm—I'm—"

As the record skipped, the girl, with every repetition, bumped furiously at the audience. After a couple of dozen skips and bumps, my grandfather would nudge the record player arm over the crack. The act was the highlight of the show.

"One day a classy lady came into the club," said my grandfather. "She watched the dancers and left. A week later, she came again. After that, every week on the same day—I think it was a Wednesday—she was there. She always sat in the same place, off to the side, near where I worked the record player."

She was young and slim, and she had a beautiful triangular face.

"The kind of lady you see in the window when you're passing a restaurant and she looks so perfect and so lovely you fall in love with her and remember her for the rest of your life," said my grandfather.

A month after she started coming to the club, she gave my grandfather a note for the Bessie Smith stripper. My grandfather took the sealed blue envelope backstage. When he returned to his seat by the record player, the beautiful lady was gone.

After every Wednesday show for the next two months, the beautiful lady gave my grandfather a note to deliver to the stripper. She never waited for an answer. My grandfather never knew what was in the notes.

One day, along with a note, she asked my grandfather to deliver a gift-wrapped box about the size of a cigarette pack. My grandfather, curious, hung around as the stripper opened the present. Inside was a ring: a small star sapphire, which she held up to the light to show my grandfather the reflected cross within the clear blue stone.

The beautiful lady stopped coming to the show, and the stripper wore the ring all the time, even while she danced. One day, the stripper came to work without the ring. During the show, the beautiful lady arrived. She sat down at the back of the theater. My grandfather, leaving the record player in charge of a friend, went to her and asked if she wanted him to bring a note backstage. She said no. The show ended. She left. My grandfather never saw her again.

"That's not a nice story," said my mother.

"Why isn't it nice?" my sister asked.

"Should I have left it out?" asked my grandfather.

"No," said my father. "They don't understand."

"I do," I said.

"What?" my sister asked.

"The beautiful lady was angry with the dancer because the dancer lost the ring," I said.

"See," my father said to my grandfather.

"Then what?" I asked.

"Someday when you're older I'll explain it to you," said my grandfather, who had hidden, in his promise to me, a promise to my father that he would be around in the future to tell me; he would not abandon my father again.

In 1934, my grandfather returned to Providence and, desperately wanting to wed himself to the arts, borrowed $1,000 from his brother-in-law Frank, who had survived the stock market crash by investing in apartment houses and finally was ruined because no one could pay any rent. My grandfather bought a used Packard touring car and started a literary magazine, *The Rhode Island Vortex.* He wrote fierce letters to dozens of established writers, promising editorial probity and high pay. The only answer he received was a five-line poem by Ford Maddox Ford, which my grandfather misplaced, so it was not printed in the first issue.

When the magazine failed—the second issue never left the printer because of unpaid bills—my grandfather moved into a cottage near Narragansett Pier with his coeditor, a cheerful Brown University graduate student named Miriam Apfelbaum, whom he had met in a used book store. On weekends, they would visit Pauline, and the three of them would spend days playing pinochle.

"How could you do that?" my mother asked my grandmother. "Weren't you furious?"

"No," said my grandmother. "I could never get angry at Aaron. He made everything—even the terrible things—seem like such an adventure. And he always meant well."

In 1937, my grandfather left them both and, having settled in Manhattan, worked for nine years in a burlesque theater as a stagehand and then stage manager.

"I spent the war adjusting pasties," my grandfather said.

When the theater was sold, gutted, and turned into a discount furniture store in 1946, my grandfather went home to Pauline. He peddled insurance, hawked balloons and kewpie dolls at parades, was doorman at a private club (one Christmas, George Raft sent him a carton of Scotch), and, at last, prompted by his brother-in-law, became a butcher—to pay off his debt; because he was tired.

The first night of our visit to my grandparents' house, I stayed awake, listening to the angry sounds from downstairs: the murmur, getting louder and louder, the hiss as everyone shushed each other, the belligerent murmurs again.

The window was open. I smelled oil and burning leaves. The few cars that passed, their motors revving, slowing as gears were changed, revving again farther off and quieter, neatly filled the silences from downstairs. I sucked on a poppy seed that was wedged painfully between two back teeth. My mouth tasted garbagey from the cabbage we'd had for dinner.

When my sister's bed creaked, I asked, "What do you think they're fighting about?"

She mumbled something jammed with lazy vowels and then, sitting bolt up, said, "Go to sleep." Throwing herself back onto the mattress, she yanked the covers over her head. Slowly, they billowed down to outline her body.

"I like him," I said aloud.

She didn't answer, so I flopped onto my back and stared at the picture that hung over my bed: a reproduction of Jacques Louis David's painting of Homer reciting a tale to some Greek youths in a marble hall. The only place I had seen people in togas before was in Flash Gordon movies, so, in my drowsy fancy, the scene struck me as classic science fiction: an elder of Betelgeuse warning the cosmic council about the invasion of Alpha Centauri locust-gods.

Through the open window near my head, like the hesitant touch of my mother's hand when she groped for signs of fever on my brow, intruded the skinned smell that comes before rain. It left me with the feeling of dipping my head into a sinkful of icy water, the cold cap that clasps the skull, the ache in the mysterious region that could be behind the eyes or at the base of the jaw.

I dreamed of wolves and death rays and my grandfather, looking like Homer, swooping up the porch steps, his arms spread into bat wings.

"The Song of the Plains," sung by the Red Army Chorus, woke me at dawn. I climbed from bed and went barefoot to investigate. In the next room, my father was honking in his sleep. His white shirt lay in the doorway like a stiff pudding. There were red ink spots above his pocket where his pen points had rubbed. From the end of the hall, I heard my grandmother smack her lips as though she were tasting, testing her sleep. There was no carpet on the stairs, and the cold treads made my feet curl.

In the kitchen, which smelled of linseed oil and last night's cabbage, my grandfather, his brown pants held up by suspenders that looped over a bare, white, hairless chest, was squeezing oranges in a juicer. When I walked in, he straightened up and, gesturing with a dripping rind, said, "Tovarich."

Having wiped his hands on his thighs, he led me

into the living room to the old-fashioned Victrola. The small doors at the bottom of the machine were open, and from the spaces between the horizontal slats, issued the ghostly swish of the needle whispering around the record's center.

"What would you like to hear?" he asked. "Chaliapin? Nellie Melba? Caruso?" He slipped a record from an album that had on its cover a picture of a red-and-white-striped swastika-ed worm being impaled by a dagger. "Robeson."

"The Four Insurgent Generals" crackled from the cabinet:

> *One Christmas, holy evening,*
> *One Christmas, holy evening,*
> *One Christmas, holy evening, mamita mía,*
> *They'll all be hanging . . .*

In the kitchen, my grandfather gave me oranges to slice. I handed him halves, which he squeezed with vicious twists of the wrist as he boomed along with the 78:

> *Madrid, your tears of sorrow,*
> *Madrid, your tears of sorrow,*
> *Madrid, your tears of sorrow, mamita mía,*
> *We shall avenge them . . .*

The table was running with juice. I was sticky up to my elbows.

When the record ended, my grandfather, wiping the backs of his hands on his rump (with his elbows out, he looked as if he were playing rooster), lumbered into the other room. I heard him crank up the Victrola, change records. He strolled back into the kitchen, his lips compressed, punching the air on the heavy musical beats.

We are *the peat-bog* sol-*diers,*
Mar-*ching with our* spades . . .

"Drink," said my grandfather, raising a glass. Strands of pulp clung to the rim. "To the Revolution. May it be short and bloody."

I grinned at his abrupt solemnity.

"When I was your age," he said, "the cossacks burned down our synagogue. Have you ever seen anything like that? Stand up. Let me feel your muscle." He pinched my upper arm until it hurt. "Flex. Flex. What're you afraid of? Hey, punch me in the gut. Go ahead. Punch me." He raised his hands as though I were sticking him up. His belly heaved over the top of his pants, round as a globe, drum-tight. Hitting it was like belting a soccer ball. "Now, you."

I mimicked his motions, raising my hands above my head; and I tried not to clench my fingers in fear.

"Ready?" he asked.

"Yeah," I said. I leaned back so my belly would bulge.

He shook his head.

"Not that way," he said. "Make your belly into a fist."

Holding my breath, squinting, I tensed my stomach muscles. My grandfather drew back his right arm—his hand palm-up—and curled his fingers over. "On your mark, get set . . ." His poke sent me sprawling.

I couldn't breathe. I felt as if a rod were being forced down my throat. My saliva tasted of onions and chocolate. I was sitting in front of the stove. When I raised my head, I cracked my skull on the oven door handle.

"You're tough," said my grandfather, "but you've got to get tougher. If they think they've hurt you, you don't have a chance."

His suspenders were dangling by his legs, and he was buttoning on a red wool shirt.

"Come on," he said, "get up."

He lifted me with one hand and set me on wobbly feet. Shrugging on his suspenders, he strode across the kitchen.

"I'm going to put on 'Volga Boatmen,'" he said, wagging a raised forefinger at the ceiling. "Be dressed by the time it's over."

Through the lofty doors, like temple doors, like doors of the courts of law, we strode, I proud of my grandfather, who wore a long leather vest and a bashed bowler, he proud of his grandson, who, in an Ivy-League, button-down, off-white shirt, was proof of his progeny's secure Americanism. All around us hung the yellowish and blood-caked carcasses of cows.

"You will eat, you will eat, by and by," sang my grandfather grandly, "in that glo-rious land in the sky wa-ay up high . . ."

Each side of beef was speared on a hook; each hook hung loose between two metal rails; the rails ran the length of the warehouse. A huge man in a blood-spattered apron embraced the suspended meat, swung it back, and sent it sailing down the room. The ball that held the hook chattered in its track. A hundred feet away, another aproned giant caught the side of beef and swung it, sending it further down the room.

The first man had grabbed another carcass and flung it on. One by one, the corpses rushed past us.

". . . work and pray, live on hay," my grandfather bellowed, "you'll have pie in the sky when you die-ee-aye . . ."

"Hey, Aaron," said a white-haired man with a scar that curled across his cheek and over his upper lip, "who's the kid?"

"My grandson," said my grandfather. "He's a good boy, Max."

Max grabbed my hand in his fist.

"You gonna be a butcher like your grandpop?" he asked.

"Butcher!" my grandfather shouted. "Butcher? He's going to be a poet."

Max stood sideways and turned his head to look down at me over his shoulder.

"Aw," he said, "whaddaya want? Waste a big kid like that on books?"

"Another Pushkin," my grandfather boomed, the name exploding in his mouth like a wind: *"Pboosh-kin!"*

Max, bending down, asked me, "You wanna be a poet, hey?" His sour breath smelled of meat loaf and milk. "Aaron, I got something to clear your brain."

Shuffling along the sawdust-covered floor, Max led us to a small, glassed-in room. The walls, partitions, extended only halfway to the ceiling. The sweetish smell of blood and dead flesh was stronger in the enclosed space.

There was a desk, covered with tissue-thin papers spilling out of manila folders, a file cabinet, one side of which was painted black, a swivel chair and three wooden folding chairs, a broken fan (the cage around the blades hung oddly forward), and a cardboard box, used as a wastebasket, filled with balls of paper, crumpled Hershey wrappers, an old girlie calendar from Anderson's Gardens, a broken milk bottle.

Max yanked open a desk drawer, took out a bottle of applejack and three dirty coffee cups, which he shook above the box. Beige liquid dribbled onto the calendar picture: a naked girl, sitting with her legs tucked under her and holding a basket of fresh fruit over her lap. Because I had never before seen a picture of a naked woman, I pulled it out.

"Let me wipe that off for you," said Max, grabbing it. Unsure whether to let me have it or, under some professional pretext, to rediscover its value and slip it into hiding, he looked to my grandfather for a clue.

"In our family," said my grandfather, annihilating the nine years of my parents' marriage during which he'd had no contact with his son, "we keep nothing hidden. I see no reason why Dennis shouldn't have the calendar."

After Max returned it to me, I rolled it up and shoved it into my back pocket.

"He's got my blood in him," said my grandfather.

"Does he?" Max asked. He poured the three cups

full of applejack, nudged one toward my grandfather, sipped from another, and nodded at the third. "Kid," he said, "drink up. You don't wanna shame the old man."

"Old?" said my grandfather. He leaned across the desk. "Do I look old?"

Max elaborately scratched his nose.

"Look," my grandfather stood up, "look at that belly. That's not an old man's belly. Come on, hit me. Hard as you can."

Max, smiling at me, made a hitchhiking gesture toward my grandfather.

"Hit me," my grandfather shouted. "I've got the belly of a twenty-year-old."

My grandfather's brag, despite its thunder, betrayed the preoccupied ease of a ritual, as though in the center of his shout loomed a yawn.

"Me," said Max, "I couldn't do it. I'm an old man too. But I'll tell you what . . ." Because I was present, Max acknowledged the challenge he normally ignored. His sense of sly justice demanded that my grandfather for my sake had to make good his boast. At the door, he called, "Reigel. Hey, Reigel, come here."

The first guy we had seen handling the meat turned and nodded, waved, loped toward us.

Quietly, he shut the door and waited. He was as tall as my grandfather, as broad, and thirty years younger. Beads of sweat, like rivets, dotted the right side of his forehead. His eyes were clear blue. When he opened his mouth to pick between two teeth with a thumbnail, I saw a crimson palate.

Max jerked his head toward my grandfather and said to Reigel, "Punch him in the belly."

"In the belly," my grandfather repeated, pointing to his belt.

Reigel put out his left hand, walked toward my grandfather until he was an arm's length away, dropped into a crouch, and, ducking his head professionally, swung.

My grandfather winced, forced back his shoulders, squinted, and gasped. His mobile grimace kept trying to become a smile. He spoke in a tight voice:

"Like a twenty-year-old."

He made jerky bows like a mechanical soldier with a sprung spring.

He said: "We got to go."

Reigel asked, "That all?"

Max said, "Yeah. Thanks."

Reigel left, again carefully closing the door.

"I'll send the meat to the store," said Max.

"Fine," said my grandfather, "fine, fine."

When my grandfather opened the door, Max grabbed my elbow and handed me the bottle of applejack.

"Give your grandpop a shot," he said, "when he feels better."

I ran after my grandfather, who was striding quickly through the warehouse toward one of the exits. By the time I got outside, he was leaning over the street, puking. He held his forehead with one hand, the back of his neck with the other. A strand of tan spittle hung from the corner of his mouth. When he straightened up, the loose end of the strand swung over and attached itself to his vest. I sat on the curb a few feet away, holding the bottle on my left knee.

He wiped his lips with his sleeve.

"Let's take a walk," he said.

As we wandered through the streets, he whistled a few notes, belched, patted his belly. I trotted beside him, carrying the bottle by its neck as though it were a bell. On a pier, he stopped, stretched his arms above his head, and asked, "Do you want to rest?"

"I'm not tired," I said.

He scowled: "I am."

We sat on the end of the dock, our legs dangling over the gray water. I unscrewed the top of the bottle and, thinking it would please my grandfather—"He's got my blood," he had said—I took a swig.

"I'm not ashamed of getting old," said my grandfather. He spat into the sea. "I've got my family now. I'll sit in my slippers and play chess with your father; and, if anything happens, you'll protect me, won't you, Dennis?" He took the bottle from me and, after wiping the top with his palm, said, "To the Revolution."

I agreed: "To the Revolution."

He howled with laughter. Standing up, he drank the rest of the liquor—I watched, fascinated, as his Adam's apple jiggled up and down—and flung the empty bottle into the water. It bobbed, leaned over, and rolled with the motion of the waves.

When we went home, we found my father standing in the dining room, his right shoulder hunched up as he talked on the telephone. After glancing at us, he quickly said into the mouthpiece, "Never mind. They just came in." He dropped the receiver into its cradle and, coming toward us, called, "Ethel."

My mother appeared in the kitchen doorway, holding a wet half-naked potato in one hand and a peeler with a curl of potato skin dangling from its jaws in the other.

She walked to my grandfather and, threatening him with the potato, said, "You weren't in the store." She wrinkled up her nose and looked at his chest. "What have you been drinking?"

My grandfather waved her away.

"We went to the market," he said.

She grabbed his arm.

"What have you been drinking?" she asked.

"Where did you go?" asked my father.

"To the market," I echoed.

My parents seemed less interested in answers than in questions, as though the fears that had hulked around their imaginations while we were gone had left them in awe of their ability to conjure up wonderful disasters. With their finicky, shallow probes ("Where did you go? What did you drink?") they were trying to sound the depth of their distrust of my grandfather. They wanted answers that would not only calm their apprehension of the morning, but heal the breach between my father and his father. That's what they had come to Providence for. Their anger was at their own mistrust. Their panic was at the recognition the mistrust might be well founded.

"Open your mouth," my mother said to me.

I kept my lips shut.

"Open your mouth," said my grandfather.

I did. My father, misreading my expression, said, "That's right, Dennis, he's betraying you."

If I looked surprised, it was because my grandfather's "Open your mouth" had been so comforting. I had only known him, after all, for less than a day. Although I liked him, I had not realized how much I trusted him. I knew I would not have opened my mouth for either my mother or my father.

"What have you been drinking?" my mother asked me.

"Applejack," said my grandfather. He coughed and added, "It's like apple juice."

"It's not apple juice," said my mother.

"It's like apple juice," I said.

My father made a step toward me, patting the air in a "Calm down, don't antagonize your mother" gesture. Understanding that my grandfather was under attack, and wanting to dramatize my support of him, I willfully interpreted my father's action as threatening. I shouted, "Don't touch me," and for protection ran to my grandfather, who dropped his hands over my shoulders.

My father stopped, and the long verticals of his face slowly wrinkled up until the lines were horizontal. It was as though he had been transformed into a stranger. I no longer recognized him, and his strangeness was thrilling.

My mother, afraid of the sudden silence that signaled the eruption of something she had been trying to avoid, fixed on the rolled calendar stuck into my pocket. Her concern and the typical quarrel she was encouraging were strategies to evade what was beginning to happen.

"What's that?" she asked me.

"Max gave it to me," I said.

Having dropped both potato and peeler into her apron pocket, she unrolled the calendar.

"Moses," she said. "Look."

"I just took him on an outing," my grandfather said.

"Moses," my mother repeated. When my father, who was still gazing at my grandfather, didn't answer, she said, "I can't handle this." Dropping the calendar on the piano bench, she slammed into the kitchen.

My grandfather sat on the couch. My father picked up the calendar and gave it to me.

"You know your mother loves you?" he said.

I nodded.

"You know I love you?" he said.

I said, "Yes."

My father glanced at my grandfather and then said to me, "Good."

My grandfather accepted this demonstration of filial love as a rebuke and, given what he assumed was a lack of any positive bond between my father and him, a punishment.

"I only took him on an outing," he said.

My father sat next to him on the couch and, leaning back, rubbed his face with both hands.

"It was a good thing to do," my father said. He made a meaningless gesture—half waving, half grasping—which he turned into a forehead scratch. "I'm jealous. You never took me on an outing."

My grandfather's expression did not change.

"Did you?" my father asked.

My grandfather thrust his hands into his pockets and jingled coins and keys.

"Did you?" asked my father, his voice rising.

My grandfather looked sideways at the hassock beside the couch.

"Answer me!" my father shouted. "Will you please answer me!"

My grandfather did not answer.

My father stood up. After glancing around as though puzzled, he left the room and walked out onto the front porch, letting the screen door slam behind him. He rapped on the window and shouted, "Sorry."

My grandfather did not acknowledge him, so my father unfolded one of the porch chairs and sat down. Having leaned over to fix a disarrayed pant cuff or tie a shoe (all I could see through the glass was the irregular curve of his hunched back), my father settled more comfortably in the afternoon chill.

Without looking up, my grandfather said to me, "There's an envelope inside the piano seat."

I lifted the top of the seat and found sheet music from a Cole Porter play, an empty but uncrushed Camel cigarette pack, two cloth BandAids, and a nine-by-twelve manila envelope, which I brought to my grandfather. He bent up the metal clasps and spilled out papers and photographs. After shuffling through the clutter on his lap, he slipped out a snapshot of a lanky, gawky man who was sitting on a grocery wagon and holding an infant in his arms. My grandfather studied the scene and said:

"That's me. That's your father. We were on an outing." And he shot a triumphant look through the window at my father, who sat turned away from us on the porch, mouthing Russian vowels.

Five

While sleeping on the bus trip from Springfield to New York City, I had burrowed in my dreams through eighteen years and discovered, like a subterranean city, a fully furnished memory: I am twelve years old and, kneeling on my bed, am ripping articles from magazines as though I were tearing the wings off birds. The loose pages flutter down; and, having left the bed, I wander through the house looking for file folders, so in imitation of my father I can sort and save my articles. In his desk, I find three empty folders, which I take; but I need more, and relying on my father's sacrificial generosity, I ransack his file cabinet, slipping out every other file folder and leaving the papers that the folders had contained in order in the drawer.

"Why?" my father asks when he discovers what I have done. "I've had those files twenty years."

"Everything's still in order," I explain, surprised at how upset he is and troubled by the realization that I have disrupted more than a file system. "I just took a few folders."

"But they're mine," my father says, his fixed grin

growing. He sucks in his lower lip, and his eyes narrow to dark arcs, the shape and color of dirty fingernail clippings. "You had no right."

To encourage Hannah's and my curiosity, my father had placed no limits on our monkeying around. When I was six and an uncle asked my father why he let me fiddle with the hi-fi he had just built, my father said he would rather have a broken record player than a dull kid—a story my uncle used to repeat with horror, claiming my father, permissive and socialistic, was not teaching his children the value of private property. I suppose he wasn't.

For the first time, standing in my father's study in front of the rifled file cabinet, I—and perhaps my father—discovered there were boundaries that enclosed a private zone he had never before acknowledged; and this knowledge distressed me, because my father always had defined his love for me as the openness of his world to my exploration. I had looked into his life as though peering through a window at an exposed landscape; suddenly objects hidden to the right and left of the frame began to cast indecipherable shadows.

Because I had assumed my life was open to his inspection the way I had thought his was open to mine, when I found that he had mysteries, I realized that I must have been equally mysterious to him, which both scared and excited me. By filching the file folders, I inadvertently had proved that I could invade his private world, exercising a power I had not known I possessed; but, if I could attack him, he could attack me. We were both abruptly vulnerable, so I prepared my defenses; and, by the time my father had repaired his expression, I understood that his fixed smile was not just evidence of pain. It was also a weapon.

I did not want my father in his room at the hotel in New York to treat me to this fixed grin—an expression made horrible by the collapsing arches of wrinkles over his eyebrows, wrinkles that normally made him look humorously surprised by life—because it would indicate he had resumed a disguise I hoped he had junked the night he tore up our garden in Leverett.

When I knocked on the door of my father's hotel room, he shouted, "Don't you see the sign?"

Dangling from the doorknob was a blue tag, which said:

Notice: Guests not desiring to be disturbed by employees knocking on the door to deliver mail, telegrams, etc., are requested to hang this notice on the knob on the outside of the door and replace after use.

I flipped the tag. On the other side was the announcement, printed in large blue letters with thorny serifs that made the words look like a barrier of barbed wire:

DO NOT DISTURB

Although I am sure the way the tag was hung was unintentional, it seemed to be typical of my father to have the wrong side of the tag facing out, explaining and trying to take you into his confidence, shying from the bare statement. Or perhaps I was just looking for evidence, even improbable evidence, with which to condemn my father to the role I had invented for him.

I knocked again.

"Who is it?" my father angrily shouted.

There was a scraping like a blade on a whetstone as he slipped the chain latch before opening the door. He was dressed in copper-colored slacks and a tin-colored shirt, a tight curl of gray hair like a cigar ash lying in the V of his open collar. He had let his beard grow, a heavy four-day mat, blue-gray like a fuzz of lichen. And the hair on his head was cropped close to the scalp. He looked at me as though I were an acquaintance who had greeted him in Times Square, someone he vaguely recognized, but couldn't place.

He put his right hand against his brow and drew it back over his head as though he were pushing off a wig. In our silence, I heard the whisper of the newly cut bristles scratching his palm.

"What do you want?" he asked.

"Aren't you surprised?" I asked, myself surprised that he was shrugging away my presence and pleased that he was scowling and that his eyes, instead of waning crescents, were dark double moons.

"I wish you hadn't come," he said, rubbing the flap of skin under his chin, trying to erase his flesh. "A friend's visiting."

When I looked behind him, he said, "She's in the bathroom."

He let me enter the room, then closed and locked the door behind us. The bed was rumpled. On the bedside table was a half-empty bottle of Wilson's whiskey, which my father claimed was "the workingman's whiskey," and two used glasses.

"We were having a drink before I go to meet grandpa," he said. And he blushed, as much, I think, because in our family "grandpa" always meant my mother's father, not my father's father, as because of the woman hiding in the bathroom. "I wish you hadn't come," he said again.

"I didn't want to," I said.

"I'm not ready to go home quite yet," he said, scratching his forehead as though the casual gesture would keep his words from sounding like a challenge.

"Can we talk?" I asked.

"About what?" he asked back.

About us. About families. I realized I had come to him not only to deliver a message from my mother, but also to ask his advice, which I had always distrusted. Usually, when I did want his opinion, it was only to disagree with him. But his running away gave him an authority he had lacked or I had with few exceptions never recognized. I wanted him to answer a question his flight had framed, but I did not know how to explain this to him. I felt myself, embarrassed by my confusion, slipping into the vagueness that I hated in him.

"I'm in a hurry," my father said.

I stared at the television set. The sound was off. The picture was on. A comic was strutting on a stage, gesturing to an off-camera audience. I tried by withdrawing my attention from the conversation to diffuse my father's narrowing anger, which, because I felt it was justified, frightened me.

"Do you have anything to drink?" I asked.

He waved at the bottle, which he knew I had seen, and, leaning over, one arm akimbo, picked up his tie from the floor. At the mirror above the bureau, he flipped his collar, looped his tie over his neck, folded the collar down, and, holding both ends of the tie, pulled it back and forth to adjust it before making a knot. I could see him watching me in the mirror as he fiddled.

On the floor next to the bedside table was a bottle of ginger ale. I poured some into one of the dirty glasses. The thin chains of bubbles hanging in the soda looked like metal filings.

"Are you afraid of getting drunk?" my father asked.

He added whiskey until my glass was full. The liquor pouring into the ginger ale looked viscous like small sheets of Saranwrap waving in the soda.

He poured himself a drink, half whiskey, half ginger ale, and took two large gulps.

"Are you surprised?" he said, turning around the question I had asked at the door.

I nodded.

He sat on the bed, put his glass on the floor between his feet, and bent over, his elbows on his knees, as though he were reading auguries in the liquor. When he looked up, he was wearing his mask: scared eyes and fixed grin. Trying to explain and excuse everything, he said, "I'm drunk."

His face, despite the beard or perhaps because of it, looked gaunt.

"Are you sick?" I asked, thinking he was all right and wasn't that drunk. I was convinced he was using his age and the possibility he might die as a shield to protect himself from me. And then I was not so sure. Maybe, while looking in the mirror one morning in Springfield, he had seen the same thing I just glimpsed, and that's why he had run away.

"You shouldn't know about this," he said.

"Can I meet her?" I asked.

"You're angry because of your mother," he said.

"No," I said.

"I don't believe you," he said.

"When I was in high school," I said, "and one of your friends got in trouble with a student—"

"Polishook," he said.

"I think it was him," I said. "You told me a father should never let his son know he's been unfaithful."

"Now things'll never be the same, huh," said my father, prophesying from his drink.

"I always thought you were admitting something to me back then by bringing the subject up," I said.

After a pause, my father said, "I'm embarrassed, but I'm not ashamed."

I pictured his girlfriend sitting on the edge of the tub as Maxie used to, before we were married, when we would have fights in hotel rooms and she would retreat to the bathroom to cry.

"You're proud I found you with her, aren't you?" I said.

"Yes," he said.

The bathroom door was ajar. I pushed it open.

She turned—as though surprised, although she could not have been—with one hand touching the towel rack and the other hand moving to her mouth.

She was wearing a yellow dress with a pattern of darker yellow giraffes. Her feet were bare.

She was older than I had expected, thirty-five? thirty-eight? and attractive in a wide way. Everything about her, hips, breasts, smile seemed to stretch generously as though she were poised on the edge of an embrace. She was what my mother would have been like, ten or fifteen years ago, if she had been happier. Two smiles, one inviting trust, the other begging for approval, warred on her lips. This flickering expression seemed to be, not a particular reaction to our awkward introduction, but a nervous habit.

"Dennis," said my father from where he sat on the edge of the bed, "meet Carla."

I could see Carla and my father, but they could not see each other.

Outside the room, in the corridor, a vacuum cleaner was humming two notes, a loud high one and a soft low one, over and over again as it was pushed and dragged across the carpet.

"About fifteen years ago," she said. Her voice was hoarse. She cleared her throat. "I was twenty-two. We taught at the same school."

She came out of the bathroom. The giraffes on her dress galloped through the pleats as she moved. I stepped aside to let her pass. She crossed the room and sat on the bed, her shoulder touching my father's shoulder.

My father, uncomfortable in my presence being so close to her, leaned back away from her on the bed, and then, feeling that was even worse, left the bed and sat in the desk chair.

"We used to make love in the supply room," she said, following my father.

Standing in front of him, she took his hands and held them to her hips.

"We'd get undressed and lie on the floor on top of our coats," she said.

"Don't tell him those things," said my father, pulling his hands away.

He tried to stand and edge by her, but she did not move. He gave up and sat there, miserable, as she took his hands and again held them to her hips.

"When he didn't divorce your mother," she said, "I never wanted to see him again. I didn't hate him. I still loved him. But I didn't like him anymore. I felt like someone in that song, you know, on the radio. I didn't want to be with him, but I couldn't help myself. That's why I came to New York."

"Did Mom know?" I asked.

"She knew fifteen years ago," said my father.

"Now?" I asked.

"No," he said. "How is she?"

"She's turned the house upside down," I said. "She needs you."

"And you're the bait to lure him back?" asked Carla, still facing my father, still holding his hands to her hips.

"No," said my father. "He's trying to scare me."

If I had been trying to scare him into going home, it was because I trusted fear more than love. I did not think he loved me enough for me to be an effective bait. And my love for him was diluted, like water widening an eye of oil, by my love for my mother.

"I feel like a traitor," I said.

"Men have to stick together," said Carla, her back almost as expressive as her face must have been. She straightened her shoulders the way people do when they are about to enter a room where they know they are going to get into an argument. "After all, someday you might want to leave your wife."

"His wife's got nothing to do with this," my father said.

After what had happened in the stream behind the farmhouse, my father did not want to talk about Maxie.

"Is she so precious?" said Carla, suddenly angry at my father.

She thought he was protecting Maxie and, in doing so, was dividing women into those who suffered—from being the agents or victims of unfaithfulness—and those who didn't. My father, however, was only protecting himself.

"You shouldn't feel like a traitor," he told me, ignoring Carla. "Nothing you can do will make me go home."

"What right do you have coming here and judging us anyway?" said Carla, refusing to be ignored. "Are you so perfect? Haven't you ever fucked anyone else?"

"It's none of her business," my father said.

"Twice," I said.

"It's none of my business," my father said.

Carla hunched her shoulders as though she were trying to keep from shivering. She still had her back to me.

"Am I his business?" she asked my father.

"I don't want you to go home if you don't want to," I told my father, trying to keep him from fighting with me, and Carla from fighting with him. I suddenly felt solicitous of us all. I did not want us to hurt each other.

"I didn't leave because of her," my father said, mistaking my concern for approval of his affair with Carla, and wanting to explain that his running away was not the result of something as simple as sexual frustration. He wanted my approval, but not if it was based on a misunderstanding. He saw Carla—I think—as irrelevant, an episode. He couldn't understand why I saw her as a central fact.

"Are you going to stay with her?" I asked.

Carla dropped my father's hands and turned to face me. My father escaped from the chair and, gently moving her aside, went back to the bed, next to which he had left his whiskey. He picked up the glass and took a drink. Carla sat in the chair my father had vacated.

"I remember one night in college," said my father. "I was walking home from the library. It was cold, and there was snow on the ground. I suddenly felt everything was possible. I don't know how to explain it. Everything seemed simple. In a way, everything has been simple. I've always gotten what I wanted. But I've always been disappointed."

I waited for him to say more, but he didn't. His silence was like a traveling crack in a picture window. I felt a tingle of panic as though my arms and hands were falling asleep.

"I don't think you answered his question," said Carla.

"Maybe I should come back tomorrow," I said.

"Stay and see your grandfather," said my father.

"Your son may not want to hear the answer to his question," said Carla, "but I do."

My father picked up his coat from the floor near the bureau where it had been tossed and shrugged it on.

"I want a drink," said Carla.

"Have mine," I said. "I don't want it."

"We can share," my father told Carla, handing her his glass, trying to make up for having abandoned her on the bed, for resisting her when he was sitting in the desk chair, for avoiding her question now.

"I'll take Dennis's," she said.

It was the first time she had mentioned my name, and it sounded almost intimate, as though by saying it she had allowed a subtle shift of loyalties to take place. When she took the glass from me, she touched my hand.

She sipped and said to my father, "I can only think of one reason why you'd be afraid to answer."

"You interrupted a conversation when you came," my father told me.

"Do you want to know what your father was saying about your mother when you knocked?" Carla asked me.

"Do you want to know what Carla was saying about herself just before that?" asked my father, louder and faster than Carla, talking over the end of her sentence.

"I only told you that to explain how lonely I was," she said.

There was something stilted about their anger, as though they had to translate what they were really fighting about into more prosaic terms in order to understand it. They seemed puzzled, not only with each other, but with themselves; and their confusion made their voices sound flat, disinterested, as if they were walking through their lines on a stage, rehearsing the quarrel for some later performance.

"I go out and pick up men," Carla explained. "Your father thinks that makes me a whore."

"I didn't call you a whore," said my father, using an English teacher's defense, trying to define his way out of the argument. "I said 'whoring around.' It's not the same thing."

"Do you want to see what your father's getting?" she asked, unbuttoning her dress.

My father grabbed her hands to stop her. They staggered around the room like two drunks dancing. Carla moaned as though she were humming a song. They slammed against a wall. My father held her hands up by the wrists like a father helping a baby to walk.

"Are you going to hold me like this all night?" she asked him.

He released her. Calmly she finished unbuttoning her dress, which she took off and threw onto the bed. Looking down at her hands between her breasts, she unsnapped the front of her bra as though she were unlocking her chest and were about to pull back the skin and muscle and expose her heart. She threw the bra onto the bed. Her nipples were dark brown, the color of wet sand, and as large as half dollars, unlike Maxie's which were pinkish and small, with narrow aureoles, almost all tip like closed flower buds.

Her underpants were Lollipops, cotton, the kind little girls wear. She pushed them down and unhooked them from one lifted foot and then the other in a comical two-step. Her pubic hair was blonder than the hair on her head, and it was curled in little corkscrews. She threw her underpants on the bed. She stood with her hands by her sides, the way models do in photographs in hygiene textbooks.

"Do you think I'm a whore?" she asked me.

"I'm going downstairs," said my father. "I'll meet you in the lobby."

After he had gone, Carla picked up her clothes from the bed and, saying "Excuse me," went into the bathroom and shut the door.

I found one of the drinks and finished it. I poured myself another and sat in the easy chair next to the bed to wait for Carla to emerge, dressed. Her stripping was not meant to seduce or shock me, but to startle a declaration of love from my father. I was surprised to realize they cared for each other.

The more my father and Carla pulled away from each other, the tighter they bound themselves, as though they were caught in one of those finger-traps that are given out as favors at children's parties. You shove your index finger into one end of the flexible wicker tube, and your puppy-lover shoves his or her index finger into the other end of the tube until your fingertips are touching. When you try to yank your fingers out, the diameter of the lengthening tube grows smaller, and your fingers are trapped. The more you strain, the firmer you are stuck. Only by relaxing can you escape.

Giddy kids, stimulated by the fever of the moment, don't want to escape. They enjoy the unyielding connection. It gives them an excuse to couple for a brief unembarrassed moment. My father and Carla, awkward as adolescents at a party and suspecting how brief their moment might be, fastened themselves together by recoiling. They were ready to ground their relationship on rancor because fifteen years before they had been unable to survive on love, although their love had been intense.

Carla's love for my father was obvious; and, although he had not gotten divorced to marry her, I think he had loved Carla more romantically than he has ever loved my mother.

When Maxie's parents forcibly separated Maxie and me a year before we finally wed, my father had consoled me by saying, "It's better not to marry someone you love too much."

"Don't you love Mom?" I had asked, irritated, not because I thought he was serious, but because I assumed he was insincere. I was sure he was trying to pacify me by saying something he didn't believe. I did not suspect he was speaking from his own disappointment until he said:

"I love your mother . . . " his voice falling on the last word as though his spoken thought had been weighted down at the end by an unspoken *but*.

"The day I married her," he continued, following

the dictates of a logic that spliced married love to resentment, "I stopped in every bar between the bus station and your grandparents' house. I wasn't ready, but the baby in your mother's belly was, so I had no choice."

While my father was telling the story, my mother entered the room; and, instead of getting angry at what I thought was a revelation, she smiled it away like an old joke.

"By the time he arrived," she said, "we had to prop him up."

She was proud of the story because it proved the strength of her attraction. She had been able to capture my father in spite of himself. But the baby in her belly had been the bait that caught them both. My mother had to believe she had trapped my father to escape the nagging fear that she too had been trapped, a worry she never quieted.

On a sunny afternoon in 1954, while my mother was ironing and watching the Army-McCarthy hearings on television, she tried to explain to me why what was happening in Washington was so important. I wanted to go outside and experiment with a rope swing I had found, the day before, hanging from an oak in Forest Park. I kept edging toward the door. Frustrated with my indifference, my mother threw the iron across the room at the couch. The electric cord ripped from the wall and snapped after it.

"Why won't someone talk to me?" she cried. "For the last thirteen years all I've done is talk to children. I don't want to waste my life like this."

When my father came home from work and my

mother told him the story, he laughed and said, "Poor Ethel."

"Don't use that tone on me," said my mother.

"That's not what I meant," said my father, no longer laughing, squinting in embarrassment. He felt trapped in a false position. He had never ridiculed any pitiable condition. He said: "I wasn't making fun of you."

"I know you weren't," said my mother, surprised at his interpretation of her anger.

She wasn't objecting to the edge of ridicule in his voice, but to the stubborn pity that dulled the ridicule. She would have welcomed mere nastiness. The concern that laced through his viciousness inhibited her. Her fury was muffled by confusion, distrust, and love. She would have given up the fight if my father had not acted as though she were too fragile to assault. By abruptly giving in to her, by trying to mollify her, he was admitting that he thought her an unequal opponent. Or so she thought.

"Your father treats me like I was a kid," she said to me, "like you."

For my father, however, pity was impersonal. He used it to block his natural and cruel irony. He pitied everyone to keep from despising them.

Once, in my first year at college, he failed to mail a book he had promised to send. More out of disappointment with his irresponsibility than anger, I telephoned to complain.

"Dennis," he said, "people are fools. Unless you're generous with them, you'll never be happy."

"You mean you're a fool," I said, bold with an hour-and-a-half drive between us.

"Yes," he confessed. "We both are."

My father readily admitted to foolishness as though, in a life of aborted projects, folly was his one accomplishment.

"I had great gifts," he once told me, "but I never used them."

Although, as I got older, I grew increasingly skeptical of my father's judgments, I never doubted this estimate of his failure, because it was one of the few realities he claimed to be sure of, and because failing greatly had a glamour that succeeding modestly lacked.

"I could have been a great trumpet player," he would say.

Or:

"After my third term as the president of the Springfield Teachers' Union," he would say, "the state office offered me the Massachusetts presidency. I turned it down. The guy who got it went on to the New England and national presidencies. That would have been me. But it would have taken too much time."

My mother was jealous of any time my father spent away from our family. She conceived of marriage as a *tableau vivant,* the contents of which she continually hinted at.

"Let's all sit around the fire," she would say as the family scattered after dinner. "Moses, we can have some sherry. Dennis, Hannah, don't you want to sit with us? Moses, where are you going . . . ?"

Sitting together before the fireplace became an obsession with my mother. She would accuse us of abandoning her, of not loving her, of being bored with her. On the nights when her accusations skidded into screams, grimly we all would cancel or delay our evening plans to gather glumly around the fireplace. After five minutes of unhappy silence, my mother would sniffle. Her scene had soured. This resentful group was not what she had imagined.

When we, unbent by her tears, would coo over her, she would sob more. Solicitousness was not what she wanted either. She wanted to be locked together in a moment when we were all, not necessarily happy, but at least content. Sitting at the kitchen table, she would gaze at pictures of families gathered around fireplaces in the advertisements of women's magazines.

"There!" she once said when I surprised her in a reverie. "Why can't we be like that?"

Because she felt shamed by the cozy banality of the advertisement, she tried to belittle her obvious envy of that fake family by exaggerating her desire. She sighed, flapped closed the magazine, and tossed it to the other side of the table.

"We'd never have any problems," she said, seriousness erupting through the slick surface of her comic tone, "if only you would all listen to me."

She wanted to manipulate us as though we were the wooden family that lay neatly wrapped in tissue in the huge dollhouse that she as a child had played with and that now sat on a table by the window in Hannah's old room.

When my father took up his trumpet again to join a local orchestra, my mother complained, "Why do you want to go out all the time? Why aren't you happy being with us at home?"

"I love you all," my father once said when he and I

sat in the kitchen after he had fought with my mother. And, making a connection I could not follow, he added, "When I was in the orphanage, I used to think if only I could get out, be on my own, life would change. Something would happen. I don't know what I wanted to happen. I just didn't want to feel the same."

And then he told me the same story he would tell me fifteen years later in his hotel room in New York with Carla listening—about walking home from the library in college, feeling that everything was possible, getting what he wanted in life, but always being disappointed.

In the hotel room, he had used that story to explain why he had run away from home. Fifteen years before—which was about the time, I now know, he was having his affair with Carla in Springfield—he must have told it to explain, to himself as much as to me, why he was not going to run away.

I was then a senior in high school and, infected by the same giddy optimism that had seized my father on his walk home from the library in college, feeling that—if only I put my mind to it—I could accomplish anything, I assumed that my father was justifying why he had settled for less than what he had wanted as a young man. Stupidly, I didn't understand that he was sketching the terrifying disappointment of achieving his goals and realizing that what he had wanted was not enough.

He had not wanted to be a great jazz musician or a union president. He had wanted to be what he was: a teacher. And he had wanted a family. But, because his success in getting what he wanted had not changed the world in the way he had expected it to change, he felt betrayed. He pitied himself for the same reason he pitied others: to keep from being engorged with hate.

At fifty years old, he collapsed from a bleeding ulcer. The teachers' blood bank was run by the rival union; and, once my father regained consciousness, he told the nurses to take the IV needle out of his arm. He refused to have what he called "scab blood" running in his veins. They had to strap him down.

When I visited him in the hospital, he told me, "The doctor says I have an ulcer because I bottle things up. He says I have to learn to express my anger. I expressed my anger. I told him I was angry about the blood they're forcing into me."

By the time I saw him, he was no longer strapped down. His rant was half in fun, but only half in fun. He had been so proud of how anger had served him as a youth, he could not understand why it had turned against him as an adult.

"It's funny," he said. A flap of almost-translucent skin at his throat pulsed in and out with his breathing. "When I was in the Home, the only thing that kept me alive was hate. Now, it's going to kill me."

But in the orphanage he had exercised his hate; as an adult, he had kept it, a prized possession, secret. Because he was terrified of ending his life as alone as he had been as a child, he never could risk expressing any displeasure, for that might turn those who loved him away.

When he ripped up the garden on our farm, I suppose it was an act of love, proof he could trust me not to abandon him if he showed how angry at me he was—something I wish I had known that night in Leverett, so, after everything, I could have gone to him and told him I loved him.

In the bathroom, Carla flushed the toilet.

"I waited for you," I called to her, wishing that I had gone downstairs with my father, so I could have had a minute alone with him.

The door lock clicked—I could not tell if she, on hearing my voice, were locking or unlocking it.

"Do you want me to go on ahead?" I asked.

"No," she called.

She came out, dressed, her make-up fixed. She asked:

"Do you think I should go?"

"Yes," I said and then, realizing that she could have meant either "go to meet your grandfather" or "leave," I said, "I think he's expecting you to join him."

She glanced around the room; found and retrieved her pocketbook, scarf, and coat; and waited for me to open the door for her. We walked down the corridor, our voices sounding either too loud or too soft. Carla said, "Tell me about your affairs."

"Even though my father didn't want me to tell you?" I asked. "Aren't you betraying him by asking?"

"He didn't want you to tell *him*," she said. "Do you think I'd betray him?"

"I was joking," I said.

"No, you weren't," she said.

"I don't know what I meant by *betraying*," I said.

"Yes, you do," she said.

"Why do you want to know about my affairs?" I asked. "To check me out against my father?"

She stepped into the elevator, waited for me to follow, and pressed the lobby button.

"Why would I want to check you out against your father?" she asked.

"So you could check yourself out against the women I've been with," I said. "One was a whore. She was very young, very muscular, and very efficient. It was like getting my teeth cleaned."

If we had not been in a closed elevator, I think Carla would have walked away from me.

"That's the kind of crack your father would make," she said.

The comparison pleased me. My father never would have said anything like that to me or anyone else in our family. It came from an arrogant part of him that he kept hidden.

"You wanted to know about my affairs," I said.

She was standing rigidly, like an animal sensing a predator, trying to blend in with its surroundings. Her skin, heated by anger, gave off whiffs of menthol, camphor, and cloves, the smell of the same cleansing cream that Maxie uses. Soured by her sweat, the smell was as sharp as mothballs, as though, until my father had come to New York and taken her out, she had been in storage.

"I wasn't trying to insult you," I said.

She nodded.

"The second time," I said, being careful how I phrased things, "was with a woman I met on a business trip."

She turned her face toward me.

The elevator stopped. She hesitated and walked out. I followed. I was looking around the lobby for my father. She wasn't.

"And . . . " she said.

"That's all," I said. "My wife and I had just moved to the country. Sort of suddenly. She couldn't stay in New York. I couldn't just drop my job, so for a month or so I came into New York a couple of days a week."

Carla wanted more.

"She picked me up in a bar," I said.

Threatened by or satisfied with that explanation, she dropped the subject.

"I don't see your father," she said. "He's probably with your grandfather. They were going to meet in the hotel bar."

I headed for the bar.

She did not move.

"None of this has anything to do with me," she said, when I went back to her. "I never should have come here."

"To the bar?" I asked. "Or to my father's room?"

"You hate me?" she said, her voice rising on the last word as though she had lifted a corner of the statement like a rug to find a question underneath. "I would if I were you."

"Did you know he was coming to New York?" I asked.

She shook her head no.

"Does he love you?" I asked.

It seemed strange, not that he was intimate with a woman other than my mother, but that he was intimate with anyone. He had always been so guarded with us.

Carla said, "I loved him fifteen years ago," as though that were an answer.

"I can't picture him as someone's lover," I said. "It's like you're describing somebody else."

Carla stiffened. In belittling my father as a lover, I was ridiculing whatever love she still had for him. I was making her, not my father, foolish.

Trying to reassure her, to accept her love for my father, I asked, "Has he changed?"

"He's gotten old," she said, an answer so obvious it could have been a rebuke, but it wasn't. He had grown old for both of us. As though humbled by his aging, we—for the moment—relaxed with each other. "When I first met him," she said, "I was just out of college, and he seemed old, but he was only in his early forties. That seemed ancient then. Now I'm almost forty."

She stopped herself. The truce was over. She did not want to confide in me. She began walking toward the bar, toward my father, who could rescue her. She had become uncomfortable talking with me, now that we no longer were fighting.

"He was distinguished," she said, her voice quickening as though she were trying to pack as many words as she could between us, "and he knew so much. He used to guess music on the radio. He never made a mistake."

"I remember," I said, recognizing my father for the first time in her description of him and wondering at the simple fact that of course he would have been much the same with her as he had been with us. She merely saw him in a different way. What she had found distinguished—his excellent ear for and knowledge of music—I had found infuriating. When he would challenge me to stump him, I would bring home records from the public library, which I would play for him, rejoicing the very few times he would make a mistake in identifying the composer or the piece. How did a game like that become so ugly? When did it turn into a nasty exercise? I was grateful for Carla's version of a habit in which my father, partly because of my attacks, no longer indulged. This imperfectly matched but nevertheless shared memory, awkwardly, temporarily linked me to her as though we had been caught accidently in the same tight wedge of a revolving door.

To separate us, Carla jammed into our conversation a memory I could not share.

"After I left Springfield," she said, "he kept calling me. Once every three or four months. Even after I got married. Even after I got divorced."

"Did you leave your husband because of my father?" I asked.

She laughed.

"I haven't been pining for your father for fifteen years," she said. "You look disappointed."

"You made me proud of him," I said.

"Because you thought he'd ruined my life?" she asked, annoyed. "I've been very happy. I am happy."

"I was proud of him," I said, "because you loved him so much."

Six

My grandfather was perched on a high stool at the hotel bar, his shoe heels hooked over the stool's top rung, his pant cuffs hitched up over purple socks, a new fashionable slouch hat—with metal rings around the band—resting on one raised knee. His eyebrows were long, but stringy and thin. White brambly hairs grew from his nostrils and ears. The underside of his chin, as flat as a frog's, glowed in the light of a candle on the bar, as though his mouth were full of fireflies. His hair, which had been white the last time I saw him twenty-two years ago, was dyed the red of raw steak. But his whispy mustache was still white. He was smaller than I remembered him.

I have never known why we did not see him after that one visit to Providence, whether it was a result of decision or drift. Every fall, my mother sent him a letter—which, every spring, my grandfather answered. My mother would read aloud his notes, no more than a line or two in surprisingly neat penmanship, the capitals large and generously looped, the small letters as exact and uniform as though tapped out on a script typewriter. They usually were jotted on the back of a post card of the Statue of Liberty, the Empire State Building, or, one year, inexplicably, a Jesus who opened and closed His eyes as you moved your head from side to side.

My father would listen, his eyebrows raised as he peered over a chess problem or his lower lip pushed out as he leafed through a book on structural linguistics (shortly after we visited my grandfather in 1949, my father gave up studying individual languages to study the nature of language). After my mother would finish, my father would read the post card over and over, and dropping it to the floor or the coffee table, would comment on the sentence structure or the use of a word: the way a present participle, because of its placement, could function in one case as a noun and in another case as an adjective. He never responded to the post card's contents.

When I married Maxie, I sent my grandfather an invitation and a letter urging him to come to the ceremony. He never answered—although in his annual note to my mother he sent Maxie and me congratulations and promised to mail a check for a wedding present, which he never did.

My father was standing at the bar next to my grandfather, talking to him and nervously tugging an ear lobe, a spy signaling his contact. My grandfather slapped the bar with the flat of his right hand and laughed, not the deep bellow I recalled, but a loud cackle that sounded like breaking crockery. My father, his arms hanging limply at his sides, made small side steps toward a table as though he were starting a Balkan line dance. My grandfather reached out, locked an arm around my father's waist—my father would have to stop edging away from the bar or else he would pull my grandfather off the stool—and waved to the bartender for more drinks. My father, impatient and frustrated, struggled free of my grandfather's grasp and raised his hands, fingers spread and palms facing inward, the gesture of a man beseeching an indifferent god. My grandfather slid off his stool. His hat dropped to the floor, unheeded. His back arched, his belly ballooning out in front of him, he held my father by the shoulders at arms' length as though they were about to tango. When I called, they both turned their intense faces toward us at the same moment.

My grandfather released my father's left shoulder (which my father reached up to massage; my grandfather's grip must have been tight); lifted his hand in a benedictory wave; and, mistaking Carla for my wife, whom he had never seen, called, "Dennis! Maxie!" Dragging my father after him, he charged across the room toward us.

He worked my right arm up and down like a man struggling with a long-unused pump and then, as an afterthought, as though to prime me with love, kissed me on the cheek. I kissed him back. He grabbed Carla in a dancer's embrace and, lightly, expertly, waltzed her a few steps until she laughed and, enjoying his antics, leaned her head on his shoulder and, smiling, closed her eyes.

He circled her back to me and spun her into my arms. I held her for a moment, not dancing. She opened her eyes, stepped away, and, angry at my grandfather for having stopped dancing with her so cavalierly, attacked him for having danced with her at all.

"I bet you sweep them off their feet at Roseland," she said.

Ignoring her annoyance, my grandfather said, "I wanted to come to your wedding," as though I had gotten married a few months, not seven years, before. "I was just changing apartments. A hectic time or I would have been there. But it's not too late to toast you now. Your seventh anniversary. First is paper. Seventh?" He scratched his upper lip with all four fingers of one hand. The nails were beautifully cared for, as glossy as polished stones set into flesh. "Something. I forget. Tenth is metal, I think. Twentieth is china. Twenty-fifth. You should know, Moses."

"Silver?" my father asked.

"Of course," said my grandfather. "Don't you remember what you gave your wife? You must have given her—what?—a silver necklace or a teapot, something."

"We don't follow those . . ." my father, uncomfortable, trailed off. "I just give her anything, whatever she needs."

"Practical," said my grandfather, "but cold. No heart. No poetry. Rituals are important. You must surrender to them. Even if they seem—what?—middle-class."

"It's a little late to start," said my father.

"Never," said my grandfather. "How long have you been married?"

My father, seeking an ally, asked me, "Dennis, how—"

My grandfather interrupted him.

"You have to ask your son?" he said. "You don't know? You should be ashamed, Moses."

"If anniversaries are so important to you," said my father, irked, "why haven't you ever sent me a birthday card?"

"Dennis," said my grandfather, turning toward me and ducking his head, as though my father's angry question had been something physical flung at him, "your wife is lovely. But you're my grandson. Of course she'd be lovely."

To Carla, he said, "You have a beautiful face, full and thoughtful. You look like you should play a lute or a mandolin. Beautiful breasts, beautiful hips. Wide hips. Good for childbearing. How many children do you have?"

Without letting her answer, he suddenly shouted at me so loudly the bartender looked up, "Plant your seed in fertile earth!" Then, more softly, but still orating, he continued. "That's what they did in the Bible, and over five millenia later we're still around. A tribe spread over the earth. I never used to believe in God, but I do now because I want to believe in the covenant. We were chosen and protected to propagate and worship. It's the opposite of human sacrifice. You worship, not by destroying life, but by creating more life. The best prayer is a fructifying fuck."

"Aaron," said my father, "this isn't Dennis's wife. This is a friend of mine. Carla."

He spoke as though her name were a coin he flipped to my grandfather.

"A friend of yours?" my grandfather said; and, when

he understood, he masked whatever embarrassment he might have felt by saying, "Carla. From Charlotte. A beautiful name."

"Carla from Carla," she said. "I never liked it."

"Dennis," said my grandfather, shying from her hostility—he seemed like an animal at bay, twisting from one attacker to another, not with snarls, but with ingratiating talk, defending himself with charm—"you look just like your father did when he was your age."

"I don't think so," I said, resenting the comparison for its easy dishonesty, and disappointed with my grandfather, whom I remembered as more heroic than this fat man spilling platitudes. "At least not in the pictures I've seen."

"Moses," he said, "doesn't he look like you did? Tell him he does."

My father, sensing my grandfather's increasing dismay, tried to make peace.

"I'd like another drink," he said; and—I suppose— because he felt he should have supported me, he offered a lesser alliance by adding, "Dennis, you'd like one too, wouldn't you?"

"Moses," said my grandfather, "tell your son he looks like you."

"He doesn't look like me at all," my father murmured. "He never did."

"A little bit in the eyes," said Carla, lightly touching below her own left eye. "And the way he stands sort of hunched like you do, Moses."

"What's the matter with you?" my father asked her. "What are you angry about?"

"What makes you think I'm angry?" she asked. "Can't I disagree with you?"

My grandfather beamed at her.

"We are right, aren't we?" he said. "Thank you."

"Do you think I said that just to make you feel good?" she asked him.

My grandfather drooped. Even his belly, which he had been thrusting out proudly as though it were the prow of a ship, sagged, a deflating balloon. His right hand with a curiously independent motion flew up and perched on his cheek. His fingers exploring the folds of flesh found a dried speck of blood crusted over a shaving nick. Carefully, as though pulling a single blade of grass out by its white root, he picked the scab away, an intimate gesture. He felt alone.

My father and I resisted him because we had been expecting something more substantial than the glib sociability with which he had greeted us. And with which we had greeted him. Carla, I'm sure, resisted him for the same reason she resisted me: she wanted my father for herself.

My grandfather was our scapegoat. Each of us was hoping to use the evening to destroy a barrier. Carla—and I—wanted to break through to my father. My father wanted to reach his father. But somehow breaking a barrier became confused with shattering a person. Before any of us would dare do more than probe, prodding each other's passions as though we were poking a stick into a zoo cage, trying to prompt some beast behind the bars to react, someone would have to crack, releasing us all from our constraints. Because my strutting grandfather seemed weakest, we had all, by meeting his vague geniality with antagonism, launched an attack.

"Let's sit down," said my grandfather.

He was buying time to collect himself.

My father and I sat on one side of a booth. Carla sat on the other side across from my father. My grandfather, who stood like a maître d' waiting for us to get settled, eased himself onto the seat next to Carla. When their bodies touched, she shifted away. My grandfather, his hands folded in front of him as though in prayer, grinned across the table at me and wiggled over until he again was touching her. She couldn't squeeze over any more. She was trapped.

My grandfather, to protect himself, had declared war on Carla. Since he, my father, and I shared the same blood, she was an outsider. Hoping my father and I would follow, he escaped from the threatening present into a memory of the only time the three of us had been together, our visit to Providence in the fall of 1949.

"Do you remember that picnic we all went on?" my grandfather asked. "At the beach? It was so cold."

"All we had was that one ratty blanket we were eating on," said my father, suddenly animated. He reached across the table and took Carla's hand. He did not want her to feel excluded. But, in describing the picnic to her, he was abandoning me. He referred to me in the third person as though I were not in the booth with them.

"I'd told Dennis and his sister about how I once went out with the Boston Polar Bear Club," my father explained, "and they decided to show me they could stand the ocean in November too."

"I don't remember," I said, joining myself in ignorance to Carla, leaving my father and my grandfather in the past.

"Sure you do," said my grandfather. "First you and Hannah tried to drag me in. No sir, I wouldn't go. You almost went in though, Moses."

He gripped my father's arm as though he were going to tug my father's hand free of Carla's.

"What did you say then?" he asked. "Something funny."

"Yes," said my father, remembering, "something about bear cubs. We used to repeat it all the time as the kids were growing up."

He released Carla's hand. My grandfather let go of his arm. My father massaged his forehead, trying to rub the memory into being.

"It was very funny," he said, dreamily, as if surprised he had ever told a good joke. He stopped rubbing his forehead and, pointing at my grandfather in humorous accusation, said, "That's incredible you remembered it."

"But I didn't remember it," my grandfather said. "Not what it was." Knowing he had succeeded in drawing my father away from Carla, he smugly told her, "I wish we could remember it for you."

"It was a long time ago," I said, resenting him for her.

"A lot of things were a long time ago," she said, and she smiled at me.

To separate Carla and me, my father, mimicking

my grandfather's method, used a scene from our past as a crowbar.

"That day at the beach," he said, "you and Hannah were so embarrassed about taking off your wet clothes and huddling under the blanket together."

My father was as successful as his father had been. Something in what he said triggered the memory, which rose in me like one of those three-dimensional cutouts—in children's books—that pop up when you turn the page. My sister and I, giggling in the back of the station wagon, had touched each other's genitals.

That memory discharged other memories of erotic encounters with my sister; how, later that fall, pretending I had hypnotized her, she had let me strip her; how, when we were older, she had walked naked into the bathroom for a shower while I was brushing my teeth; and how, when we were in high school, she had arrived home late one night after a date and, seeing that my light was still on, had come into my bedroom to tell me how her boyfriend had rubbed up against her on the front porch before letting her go inside the house. Humiliated by what had happened, she had spread the scene out for me as though it were a stained sheet she had flipped open.

"I do remember," I said.

And, as the conversation moved on, I felt left behind, disturbed and confused, in the past.

"Twenty-two years, Moses," my grandfather said. "Twenty-two years."

"I don't know why—" my father began.

"—you stayed away so long?" my grandfather interrupted.

"Why I came now," my father said.

A waitress took our orders for drinks. My father and I had Wilson's on the rocks. Carla asked for a whiskey sour. My grandfather said, "Another rum. I've drunk only rum ever since I lived in the Bahamas."

"When did you live in the Bahamas?" my father asked, his voice snagging on a laugh.

My grandfather dragged surprises from his past as though his past were a magician's top hat.

"I went there after Pauline died," my grandfather said.

He came home from the butcher shop one afternoon to find her sitting next to the stove, her legs straight out in front of her forming a V, a wooden spoon clenched in her fist. The bottom of the pan that had been left on an open flame was glowing red hot.

Two years later, my grandfather opened the walk-in refrigerator in the store to find Frank, his brother-in-law and partner, lying dead in the sawdust, curled up like a sleeping child, the back of his sweater pulled over his head.

"He must have gotten locked inside," said my grandfather. "There was no reason to stay in Providence anymore."

He sold the store and took his share of the profits to New York, where he bought pornographic magazines, which he then sold for four times what they had cost him to Elks Clubs, American Legion Halls, and other fraternal organizations in small towns all over New England.

"I'd stop the car on some back road in New Hampshire," he said, "and stare at the pictures for twenty minutes, half an hour. I'd really examine them, trying to figure out what it was that people liked, that I liked. It's not just that they were dirty pictures. There was something else in them. They somehow reminded me of my childhood, of when I was very young before I knew anything about sex. They were very dirty, but they reminded me of something that wasn't dirty at all."

Once, outside of Keene, New Hampshire, he was stopped by a police car and two other cars, full of high-school-age kids, that had no police markings. The policeman, who was almost a boy himself, twenty-two, twenty-three at the oldest, was polite, deferential. He took my grandfather into the woods and walked with him in silence over the soggy spring earth until they were out of sight of the road. He invited my grandfather to sit on a damp log, which my grandfather did. The policeman remained standing.

"We know what you're selling," he said.

When my grandfather started to answer, the policeman said quaintly, "Hush now."

After half an hour, one of the high school kids came running through the woods, calling.

The policeman asked my grandfather to stay where he was for a few minutes and followed the boy out to the road. My grandfather waited, enjoying the smell of the marshy ground and squinting up at the sky.

"Not a cloud," he said. "It was so clear and blue, you couldn't believe anything terrible could ever happen on such a day."

When the policeman did not come back, my grandfather ventured out to the road. He found his car overturned in a ditch. The wiring had been ripped out, and red paint had been poured over the motor and into the crankcase and gas tank. Red paint also had been poured over all the pornographic photographs and magazines in the car. My grandfather's suitcase was standing a few yards away, by the side of the road.

My grandfather picked it up and started walking. When he heard a car coming, he swung around and stuck out his thumb. It was the police car, driven by the policeman who had taken him into the woods. The policeman stopped the car, leaned across the front seat, and opened the passenger door. My grandfather climbed in.

"I didn't like to think of you having to walk all the way into town," the policeman said.

He dropped my grandfather at the Keene bus station.

Back in New York, my grandfather met a man named Cowper who was selling a quarter interest in a bar and small inn on Great Abaco near Treasure Cay. Small Happiness Lodge. A ramshackle building, which housed the bar, the office, and a few rooms where Cowper and his wife lived. And four cabins, not too sturdily built, with wicker furniture painted gold, iron bedsteads flecked with rust, and damp mattresses that smelled of mold.

My grandfather invested most of his savings, bought himself a white suit and a Panama hat, moved to Small Happiness Lodge, and for six months lived in one of the cabins. During the peak season, only one other cabin was occupied.

"By a young man who never went outside," said my grandfather. "Cowper's wife brought him all his meals and drinks on a tray, which she left outside his door. At the end of a week, he went back to the States. I never found out why he came or what he was doing."

Cowper's wife was a prim woman who wore her graying hair in a bun with a flower in its center. She read books that her daughter, who was in college in the United States, sent to her; and she played checkers with my grandfather. After a few months, Cowper decided she was having an affair with my grandfather. My grandfather woke up one night and found Cowper splashing gasoline over the furniture, the floor, and the bed in which my grandfather was lying. When Cowper saw my grandfather was awake, he stopped spilling gasoline and drunkenly asked, "Do you have a match?"

My grandfather left the island the next day. Within two years, the Small Happiness Lodge was bankrupt.

Back in New York, my grandfather worked in odd jobs: a waiter in a kosher restaurant, a clerk in a stationery store, a cashier in a cigar store.

"I never took welfare," he said. "When I couldn't find work, I was a model at the Art Institute. The kids there loved drawing me. A fat old man naked on a chair in a big cold room. I once got a hard-on while posing, and after class one of the girls, Nancy Harvey, asked when was the last time I'd had a woman. I was sixty-nine years old, and it had been a long time. She took me home with her."

Nancy was chubby with lovely pink baby-pads in her cheeks. She lived on East Eleventh Street between

Avenues B and C in a fifth-floor walk-up. Three dark rooms with a bathtub in the kitchen and, outside in the hall, a toilet that was shared with three other apartments. As they made love on the living room floor, she continually sniffled and sneezed because of the dust.

She made him dinner and, for dessert, served him cake because, she said, it was her twenty-first birthday. When he started to leave, she told him she had nightmares and asked him to stay. The next morning, while she slept, my grandfather swept her apartment and cooked her breakfast.

"I lived with her for a year," he said, "but we never made love after that first time."

During that year, she filled her letters to her family with hints about my grandfather to prove how happy she was and to provoke them.

"They were always telling me to dress better, to get my hair done, to wear make-up, to diet," she told my grandfather. "They said I was sloppy, I would never be attractive to men if I didn't fix myself up. You don't care if my hair's not done or if I'm not wearing lipstick."

She did not ask if my grandfather cared that she was overweight; but, if she had, my grandfather would have answered honestly that he did not care. She was young. That was all he cared about.

At the end of the year, Nancy's father, who worked for the Agency for International Development, came up from Washington to convince my grandfather to leave his daughter.

"He was twenty years younger than I was," said my

grandfather, "tall and well dressed. During dinner, he kept clearing his throat."

He offered to help clean up and, after washing the dishes, asked Nancy for some lotion for his hands.

"He was the most civilized man I've ever met," said my grandfather. "Nancy thought he was a spy."

The three of them sat in the living room. Harvey asked whether or not my grandfather intended to marry his daughter, what their plans were, how they could live together considering the difference in their ages; and then he started to laugh.

"He couldn't stop," said my grandfather. "It was terrible to see."

Still laughing, Harvey stood and left the apartment. That night, my grandfather told Nancy he was going to move out. She wept; but the next morning, when my grandfather woke, she was gone. She did not want my grandfather to abandon her; she wanted to be the one to leave—even if she had to move out of her own apartment to do so. My grandfather packed his few belongings in a shopping bag and left. A week later, he sent his set of keys to her through one of her Art Institute friends, who told him, "We're all glad she came to her senses and kicked you out."

During the mid-sixties, my grandfather worked in a theater cleaning up after rock concerts; and later, when the theater closed, he became a messenger.

"That's what I do now," he said. "It doesn't pay much, but I don't need much."

"Why didn't you go to Springfield and live with Moses?" Carla asked.

My father and grandfather, as though sharing a joke at Carla's expense, grinned.

"When I'm retired," my grandfather said, "that's when I'll go to Springfield. I'll sit on a rocker on the front porch—Moses, you have a front porch, don't you? You must—and I'll watch the leaves fall."

"Why don't you let him live with you?" Carla asked my father.

"I don't live there anymore," my father reminded Carla.

When he explained to my grandfather that he had run away, my grandfather said, "You can live with me."

Excited by his scheme, my grandfather grunted out of the booth in the virtually empty bar and paced off the dimensions of his room, describing how the furniture could be rearranged. While the bartender and waitress watched, indulgent and amused, he moved chairs together to show where the beds would be and jockied tables across the floor to represent bureaus.

"Have you run away too, Dennis?" my grandfather asked me. "We can all live together."

"I'm going home tomorrow morning," I said.

As though he had expected me to convince or force him to go home, my father asked, "Without me?"

"I don't know," I said.

"Moses, you're staying with me," said my grandfather. "And, Dennis, you'll help us get everything settled."

"I was hoping you'd come home with me, Moses," said Carla.

"How long would you want me?" my father asked.

"I thought that wasn't why you came to New York," I said to my father.

He never would move in with my grandfather, but he might move in with Carla. I had lied when I had told my father I did not know if he was going home with me. I would not leave without him.

"You can come home with us," my grandfather told Carla.

"And service you both?" she asked.

"I'm a little old for that," said my grandfather.

He sat heavily in one of the chairs he had moved to indicate where my father's bed would be placed in his small room.

Carla edged out of the booth, walked to my grandfather, and, putting her arms around his neck, perched on his knee.

"What about your twenty-one-year-old art student?" she asked.

"That was ten years ago," he said.

He put his arms around her waist to keep her from slipping from his knee.

"I'm so old and fat," he said, "I don't even have a lap anymore."

Carla took his face in her hands and kissed him on the lips. When she pulled away, my grandfather said:

"I thought you were Moses's girl."

"He doesn't want me," she said. "Will you dance with me again?"

The music piped into the bar was a slow-tempo easy-listening version of a Beatles' medley. Carla stood and held out her arms to my grandfather.

"I'll dance with you," said my father.

I slid from the booth to let my father out. He walked to Carla and took her in his arms; but, when he tried to dance with her, she would not move.

My father yanked her toward him and pushed her back, maneuvering her around the floor as though he were shifting one of the bureaus my grandfather had wanted to rearrange in his room. She hung, a dead weight, in his grasp, but she had closed her eyes and was smiling as she had done when my grandfather upon meeting her had waltzed her briefly.

Gradually, she resisted less until my father could support her with one arm. With his free hand, he stroked her buttocks. She arched back, startled; and then they kissed, a passionate peck as though they were being snapped together at the lips.

They stopped dancing.

"Are you coming home with me?" Carla asked.

"No," said my father.

Carla disengaged herself from his embrace and crossed to the bar. She picked up my grandfather's hat from the floor and put it on her head. It covered her forehead and the tops of her ears. Hoisting herself up on a stool, she ordered another whiskey sour from the bartender, who had been enjoying my grandfather's, my father's, and Carla's antics.

"I'm not going home with you either," my father told my grandfather. "Or you," he said to me. "Why do you people think I have to go home with someone? Don't you think I can live on my own?"

Watching my father caress Carla's buttocks, I had

been shocked, not by how sexual their relationship was (I had assumed their love had been based on sex), but by how asexual, how casual, familiar, and unurgent the gesture had been. They shared a congeniality that, because he was a man and she was a woman, they had felt obliged to turn into an affair. What they wanted from each other was not sex, not love, but companionship. They had danced, slowing down more and more, as though they wanted, not to press their bodies together, but merely to stand close and look into each other's face, enjoying what they saw. They were comfortable in a way my mother and father never had been.

My mother and father, trapped in their marriage, clung together as though they were spinning around in a quickening dance. As they twirled faster, they could not let go of each other without being flung into space. They were linked by a more elemental force than that which fastened my father and Carla. It was a love that could not afford the ease of friendship, a union that used to perplex me. Why, since they fought so much, didn't they leave each other?

When Maxie and I decided to marry, I used to measure our relationship against my parents' marriage and condemn them. The fights I had with Maxie seemed more vivid and less ritualized. We were not yet frozen into roles. Because we were not as dependent on each other, we could risk a purer cruelty when we fought and a ruthless love when we didn't. Maxie and I—I had been sure—would never slip into the dull continual quarrel that my parents accepted as married life.

But we did. And, watching my father and Carla flirt

angrily with each other, I was startled by a reverse perspective. The way my father and Carla struggled together reminded me of the way Maxie and I used to fight.

However, when my father sat next to Carla at the bar and, to make amends, playfully bumped his knee against hers, I recognized a tactic I had used to make up, not with Maxie, but with Abby, the woman I had told Carla about, whom I used to see when I would commute to New York during the first few months after Maxie and I moved to Massachusetts. I had accused Carla of wanting to know about my affairs in order to check herself out against the women I had been with. I was doing the same thing, comparing Carla and my father's affair to the affair I'd had with Abby, in order to measure myself against my father.

My father, in not going home with Carla, had failed her. At least, I wanted to believe he had failed her, because, in my affair, I had failed Abby. The last time I saw her, we had just returned to the apartment she shared with her mother on Central Park West when the telephone rang. After answering it, she asked me, "Would you get me a pencil and a piece of paper from my desk? This man on the phone says my sister is dead."

I abandoned my bag of groceries on the cane-bottom chair next to the front door and walked quickly down the hall to the room where, the night before, Abby and I had slept like drowning swimmers, hampered by but clinging to each other's body.

Abby had pulled her sister's bed from under the window and, having pushed it next to her own, had made both beds as one with double sheets. Pinned in two neat rows across the bulletin board that hung above the two beds were snapshots of Abby squatting among red and yellow leaves in front of the Smith College library; sitting on the steps of Dawes House in a torn white T-shirt, rolled up shorts, with a BandAid on her shin; grinning out from under a wide-brimmed straw hat as she's about to climb into a Volkswagen; and of Abby's sister leaning against a huge snow Snoopy at the Dartmouth Winter Carnival, squinting into the glare of a ski slope; and, in an underexposed photograph, plopped in a snowdrift, a thread of sunlight, as incandescent as a filament in a lightbulb, masking her eyes.

My suitcase—shirts in plastic bags, slacks, underwear stacked neatly inside—lay open on the floor. I snapped it shut and, having found a green felt-tipped pen and a pad under the clutter of resumés and job applications on Abby's desk, carried the suitcase into the kitchen, where Abby, her heels on the edge of her chair seat, her knees drawn up to her chest, was asking the man on the telephone, "What do I do now?"

Taking the pad and pen without looking at me, she wrote, left-handed, her arm hooked around the top of the paper like a child in school trying to hide her quiz answers, "Warburton's Funeral Home" and an area code 413 number.

After hanging up the phone, she told me, "I don't want to call my mother."

Abby's mother, an importer of brass lamps and marble Don Quixotes, had divorced her husband a decade earlier. The first time I visited the apartment, she had interrupted us—I was making a cup of tea, Abby was peering into the oven at a batch of brownies she was baking—and had stayed just long enough to appraise me, as though I were a statue she was thinking of buying for resale, before finding an excuse to leave the apartment so we could be alone. I suspected her of mapping out for Abby possible strategies of wooing me away from Maxie and, with an interior decorator's touch, rearranging our affections enough to transform our affair into a marriage.

Silently, I dialed the telephone number of the Bath and Tennis Club, where Abby's mother was spending the weekend; and, my heart pounding the same way it had when I called Abby the day before from Penn Station to tell her I was in town, I waited for the distant ringing to be severed by the click of the picked-up receiver.

"You can't," said Abby, taking the phone from me and turning her back to talk into it.

I waited until the switchboard operator had connected Abby to her mother's room before I left the kitchen.

At eight-fifteen, earlier that same evening, while her sister's car was skidding across the solid yellow line on Route 9 outside of Hadley, Massachusetts, Abby was waiting in the lobby of the Fifth Avenue Cinema for "Grand Illusion" to end.

"I can't take movies about war," she said, slipping back into her seat beside me in the dark.

"I thought you had gone home," I whispered.

"Are you angry?" she asked, surprised. I never had lost my temper with her before, and to ease me out of my mood, to make me feel guilty of the misunderstanding, she said, "You're afraid *I'll* leave *you?*"

The second film was about a woman who loved two men. As we left the theater, I said, "I don't believe people really get stuck in tangles like that," and we laughed because I loved Maxie and I loved Abby and I had been splitting my time between them all fall.

Abby hooked her arm through mine and watched my face. Although I no longer lived in New York, Maxie and I still had enough friends who did, to make me shy of advertising our affair. Whenever Abby touched me in public, I squinted as though by impairing my vision I could make it difficult for others to see me. When I started to slide my arm away, she tightened her grip. I would not be able to pretend that we had merely slipped apart.

"You're always trying to leave me," she said as I plucked her hand from my arm.

"If anyone saw us, we'd have to stop being together," I said, trying, as she had in the theater, to make her feel guilty for something I had done.

When I was with Abby, I felt we were slowly suffocating, as though we were living inside one of the glass eggs that Abby's mother sold in her shop. To crack open this isolation, I tried to pull Abby into my everyday world. Three weeks before my last night with her, as though I were focusing a camera, trying to merge the two ghost images in the viewfinder, I had brought Abby and Maxie together. In a many-windowed restaurant at the top of a Fifth Avenue office building, smog obscuring Central Park and part of the East Side as though I were still on the farm in Leverett dreaming imperfectly of the city, the three of us perched on our chairs like children who, having been bustled from their usual routine, waited to discover if the change were due to a festival or funeral. Having been surprised into silence by the friendliness of the introductions, we sat with our hands spread on the table as if at a séance.

When I left them to get some hot hors d'oeuvres, Maxie and Abby, released from their trance, began cautiously to chat. When I returned, they were leaned across the table toward each other, locking me out of the conversation. By denying that I linked them, they were trying to find another tie. Both had gone to Smith College although eight years apart, and both had taught elementary school. They smiled over the difficulties of finding teaching jobs in New York and western Massachusetts until Abby said, "Of course, you don't have to support yourself."

As we dropped to Fifth Avenue in an elevator that seemed to be mimicking the collapse I felt within my throat and chest, our resumed silence was interrupted by an explosion—a plane snapping the sound barrier like a whip? a revolutionist's pipe bomb?—that was doubly muted by the walls surrounding us and by the bubbles the quick descent had forced into our ears. The three of us in discomfort yawned as though the sound had wakened us from some shared sleep, and Maxie said, "Whenever I hear any kind of explosion, I want to duck under a desk the way they taught us in fifth-grade civil defense drills."

"When I was in fifth grade," Abby said, "they hadn't had civil defense drills for years."

"She's such a kid," Maxie said when we returned to the hotel where we were staying that night. "Why do you like her? Because she's young? She doesn't know anything."

"She knows different things," I said, missing, as I eased between the sheets, the familiar creak, like the sound of a door opening onto a dream, with which our old bed in Leverett always welcomed me.

"What things?" Maxie insisted.

Because I didn't want to fight, slipping into sleep as though I were sliding into a bathtub of warm water, I said, "She knows I'm not going to leave you."

And by saying that I made it true.

That last night Abby and I slept together, I had compulsively explained, "This won't go anywhere."

"Don't talk," Abby said. "You'll tell me how wonderful your life is, and I'll be jealous because mine's miserable."

"Why miserable?" I asked, feeling abruptly as I spoke that my question, like an accordion scenic post card of New York, had flipped open to reveal many questions.

"My life has nothing to do with you," she said. "Don't ever ask about it."

So, when her sister was killed, I did not ask anything. Abby hung up the phone and said, "My mother's boyfriend is driving her home. They'll be here in a couple of hours."

"I'll stay until they come," I said. Made formal by death, I stood when she entered the living room, where I had been sitting.

"This has nothing to do with you," she said; "I'll be all right."

At the front door, Abby, as though surfacing from a still pond, her face shocked open by the sudden change in elements, stretched up to kiss me on the mouth. Without waiting for me to turn away, she closed the door. When I pushed the elevator button, the surrounding glass plate lit up as if surprised by my ring.

On Columbus Circle, a few blocks from Abby's apartment, I stepped into a telephone booth and called her. When she answered the phone and asked me, "What do you want?" I hung up.

I wanted her to want me to stay. I wanted to be able to stay. I wanted Maxie to not mind my wanting her. I wanted my life to be uncomplicated. Which is why I had moved to the farm. To simplify everything.

After the affair with Abby, my life did become more and more uncomplicated, as though in ending the affair I had severed a tie, not just to a lover, but to all emotion. I would sit in a comfortable chair for hours, a cup of untouched cooling herb tea on the table beside me, staring at the slowly rising level of snow banked against the window and at the swirling storm, which dissolved the field, the barn, the line of trees, and the road in white. All that was left was the desperation I had told my father about; my lack of emotion, like a loud noise, would startle me as I sat watching winter erase the world, and my heart would beat as fast as if I just had stopped a car from skidding off an icy road into a tree.

In the spring, the rains, and the streams fed by the melting snow, and the tiny, branching rivulets that turned our driveway into mud, all that water, seemed to flush out the desperation. In the summer, I could garden or lie in the sun for hours without thinking about anything, just smelling and looking at and listening to the world—which, as I had hoped, had become uncomplicated.

But the simpler my world became, the more I felt a stranger in it, until, by the time my father arrived in the fall, circling the house and looking up at the hammock on the second-floor porch, my world had become as unfamiliar to me as it was to him.

At the bar, Carla, unwilling to be placated by my father's bumping knee, moved down to the next stool, away from him. He moved to the stool she had been sitting on. She again moved away. He again followed.

He kept glancing at my grandfather, who had retreated back into the booth. My father was playing a scene with Carla for my grandfather's benefit in the same way, upstairs in the hotel room, Carla had played a scene with me for his benefit.

Carla moved again—the last stool at the bar. My father did not follow. If he did, she might get up, end the game, and leave.

"Sit with me, Moses," my grandfather called.

My father joined my grandfather in the booth. They sat across from each other, their hands folded in front of them. My father sneezed, fished a handkerchief from a back pocket, wiped his nose, replaced the handkerchief, and once more folded his hands in front of him. My grandfather said, "Bless you."

I was standing at the opposite end of the bar from where Carla perched. She was trying to ignore me. She ordered another whiskey sour, tapped a cigarette from a pack, and stuck it in her mouth. Her teeth closed on the filtered end before her lips did. Her hand shook as she struck a match on the matchbook.

She—and then I—turned to observe my father and grandfather in the booth. Carla and I had become the audience; my father and grandfather had become the players.

"What are you going to do on your own?" my grandfather asked my father.

"What have you done all this time on your own?" my father asked in return.

"Are you going to sweep theaters or become a messenger?" my grandfather asked.

"I've been told they're not bad jobs," said my father.

Carla gave a single unvocalized explosive breathy laugh.

"I'm happy," my grandfather told my father. "Moses, isn't that what you wanted to find out?"

"I've never thought of you as ever being unhappy," said my father, who had come to New York for his own sake, not because he was worried about my grandfather. "Why shouldn't you be happy? You've always done what you wanted."

"If you had asked me to, I would've come live with you," said my grandfather, as though to prove he had not always done what he wanted.

"Why didn't you want to live with me when I was a kid?" asked my father.

"I was trying to do something," said my grandfather. "Something important, something successful, so you wouldn't have to . . ."

His voice got slower and softer like a record running down on the old hand-cranked Victrola he used to own.

"So I wouldn't have to do what?" asked my father. "Struggle like you did? I had to struggle in that damn orphanage."

"I was going to say, fail like I did," said my grandfather. "But I didn't want you to have to struggle either." He turned to me and, raising his voice as though we were separated by twenty yards, not twenty feet, asked, "You didn't have to struggle, did you?"

"My father was a good provider," I said, understanding for the first time how important that was. With the understanding came gratitude that he scrupulously had discharged his paternal duties; but, with the gratitude, I also felt very clearly the anger that had been growing all day. As much as I admired his running away from his fatherly role, I resented it.

"He waited until his children were grown before abandoning them," I said.

Carla slipped off her stool at the other end of the bar.

"I've got to leave," she said. "Excuse me."

My father jumped up.

"Don't go," he said.

"Why not?" she said. "You're too afraid to come home with me."

"That's not what I meant," said my father, annoyed at her annoyance and trying to hurt her. "Some guy might show up who you could pick up."

Carla walked to my father and slapped his face hard. When my father did not respond, she slapped his face again. And again.

"Go on," said my father.

She launched herself at him and started punching his face, the side of his head, his neck. He raised his arms to block the blows; and, making a horrible sound in the back of her throat—*howgh howgh*—like an animal in pain, she pummeled his chest as though she were pounding on a door that, if she banged long enough, would mysteriously open onto some secret chamber in which the man who loved her was hidden.

She stopped hitting him. In between gasping and sobbing, she said, "You'll end up just like your father. Old. Alone. Hated by everyone. You run away from everyone."

My father slapped her face so hard she stumbled.

"Everyone," she said. "Your wife, your son, me."

My father took a step toward her to hit her again, but my grandfather hugged him from behind, pinning his arms to his sides, holding him still.

Carla grabbed her pocketbook and left, my grandfather's hat still, comically, on her head.

My grandfather released my father, who, without turning to face him, said, "Thanks."

To me, my father said, "Make sure she gets home safely, Dennis."

I caught Carla in the hotel lobby. She was buttoning her coat with a child's concentration, her head bent over as she gazed at the stiff manipulation of her fingers. When I approached, she turned away and raised one shoulder as though it were a wing under which she was tucking her head.

I finished buttoning her coat for her.

"When he called me on the telephone yesterday," she said, "I thought—I hoped—he had come for me."

I took my grandfather's hat, put it on my head, and, guiding Carla out into the street, took her home.

Seven

After peeking into her daughter's bedroom, Carla carefully closed the door and, crossing to the wide window overlooking Riverside Park, pulled the curtains, blotting out the streetlamp light.

"When I started to live alone again," Carla said, "after my husband left me, I was terrified. I wanted to go back to Springfield, but I was too ashamed. I was sure everyone knew what had happened with your father. When my mother died, I moved some of her furniture here. So it was like going back even though I was afraid to."

I could not see her in the dark, and the following silence embarrassed me. I felt she was waiting for some kind of reassurance or at least an indication that I understood her feelings. She was bullying me with her pause.

"How old is your daughter?" I asked.

"Twelve," she said.

As though I had meant something else by my question, she added, "You don't have to worry about her. She's a deep sleeper. She won't come out."

"What's she like?" I asked. "Apart from being a deep sleeper?"

"Don't make fun of me," she said, her voice moving away in the dark.

A light went on in another room. The kitchen. Carla was bent over, peering into the refrigerator.

"Empty," she said. "A whore's refrigerator."

Inside was a quart of milk, a carton of eggs, a pound brick of butter on a saucer, and two foil-wrapped packages, which she took out. One held a loaf of bread that, she explained, she had baked herself. She stuck the bread into the oven to warm. The other held a pound of beef, which she unwrapped, put on a chopping block, and started cutting up.

"It'll cook faster in small pieces," she said. "I'm starved."

She popped a piece of raw meat into her mouth.

"Do you have kids?" she asked, the words all vowels, the consonants chewed up with the beef.

"No," I said.

"Why not?" she asked.

I didn't respond. She continued, "Leslie's not like me. She doesn't need people. She doesn't need me."

"But you need her," I said.

"You don't want kids?" she asked, her mouth full of raw meat again.

"No," I said.

"Never?" she asked.

"Never," I said.

"What do you and your wife do?" she asked.

"She uses a diaphragm," I said.

"She does all the work," she said. "That's not fair."

When I did not answer, she asked, "Why don't you get a vasectomy?" When I still did not answer, she said, "Not never."

She was right. The night before, in bed in my mother's house in Springfield, I accidently had awakened Maxie when I returned from the bathroom.

Sleepily, she asked, "You still mad at me?"

"You still mad at me?" I asked back.

We drowsily talked over the past few days' events; and Maxie, as though testing how sincere I had been in saying I did not want any children, also asked me why I didn't get a vasectomy. At the thought I might, I shivered as though an ice cube had been touched to my groin. Cutting the vas deferens was like snipping the thread tethering me to the past, freeing me as though I were a child's helium balloon that, its string snapped, would float higher and higher. I was not sure I wanted such freedom.

When I told Maxie I did not want to get a vasectomy, she said, "If you'd wanted one, I would have left you."

She reached down under the covers to arouse me. I rolled onto her and entered her. When she felt I was about to come, she said, "I don't have my diaphragm in."

Grunting with effort, I withdrew and then, controlling myself so I would not come outside of her, reentered her and came. She put her hands between our chests and pushed me up so she could look into my face.

I told Carla about what had happened between Maxie and me that night, as though it were as important for her as it was for Maxie to understand what it meant. Then I asked her:

"You like being a parent?"

"It's all I have," she said. "Leslie's my family."

She was cutting the pieces of beef into smaller and smaller chunks as though, mesmerized by the process, she would keep slicing until there were only threads of meat left. Her hands were red from the blood.

"I'm getting old," she said, making a jump from family to mortality. "Last week at a party I met a photographer about your age. And I said something, you know, that you say over drinks. He laughed and said I felt that way—whatever it was, it's not important—because it was my generation's thing."

She enclosed her story in vague phrases as though she were packing moist clay around the event, partially to hide it from me because she was embarrassed about being thought of—even in an anecdote—as being old, and partially to protect it from the changes of retelling, as if she were making a perfect cast of what had happened that night.

"It's taken me a long time to realize that when I have affairs now, I'm usually 'the older woman.' With your father, I'm not."

She stopped cutting the meat.

"I don't think I'm hungry," she said. "Do you want any of this?"

I said no.

She left the knife on the counter and, without washing her bloody, sticky hands, slipped on calico potholder mittens. Stooping, she took the foil-wrapped loaf of bread from the oven, shook the mittens from her hands, unwrapped the foil with quick plucking tugs to keep from burning her fingertips, and flipped the steaming bread over so she could knock on the bottom of the loaf like a doctor tapping the chest of a patient.

"Do you want some bread?" she asked; and, ignoring my no, she took a serrated knife from a magnetic strip above the counter. As she sawed through the loaf, she accidentally cut her thumb. Her blood soaked into the warm dough. She turned on the cold water and put her thumb under the stream. Then, she washed the beef blood from her hands. She wrapped her thumb in Kleenex, which became bright red over the wound, absent-mindedly took a bite of the soggy blood-soaked slice of bread, made a face, put the slice on the crumpled used tinfoil, and aimlessly opened and closed the refrigerator door.

"Excuse me," she said and left the kitchen.

I waited for a minute, but, worried about her, finally followed her into the bathroom, the only other room in the apartment with a light on. She was standing with her back to me, but I could see her face in the mirror. She had been crying. Her eyes were pink, her eyelids puffy, and her make-up spoiled. On her cheeks at the end of each trail of mascara was a blue-black dot where a sliding muddy tear was drying. She had wept—unlike her dry sobs in the bar—innocently, like a toddler, without rubbing her eyes.

She held up her thumb.

"I don't have any BandAids," she said.

I touched her shoulder, and she turned around and kissed me on the mouth. Her lipstick tasted soapy. Her breath smelled sour from liquor and sweet from the beef. I walked into the dark living room. She turned off the bathroom light and followed. We undressed. She lay back on the couch. I climbed onto her as though I were crawling out of a muddy stream onto a bank. She copulated jerkily, as if she were trying to throw me off, although she had linked her legs around me, hooking her feet under my calves. Our sweaty bellies slapped together like cymbals.

When we were done, Carla lay still, her breathing slowing into a regular rhythm until—I thought—she slept. Carla, aggressive while making love, when finished, retreated. Maxie, instead of jerking back and forth, makes love with her arms and legs spread. She moves in circles, so silently and gently that sometimes her orgasms pass over her like wind rippling the surface of a lake. She is more withdrawn than Carla while making love; but, when we are done, she is more open than she is at most other times. Energized by sex, she will wrestle and tumble; jump from bed (one February noon just after we married, she incited us to leap naked from our Northampton back porch into a snowbank); jabber; or, if I turn over to snooze, bustle nude about the house, washing floors or dishes, scrubbing walls, repairing chairs, digging in the garden.

When her mother once said I had changed her, Maxie protested:

"Sex did."

"You mean *love*," said Maxie's mother.

When I first met Maxie, she radiated enthusiasm for everything. She was indiscriminatingly joyful—although she remembers herself as being continually insecure and unhappy. Over the years, she has become more self-contained, less extroverted, a watcher. A collapsed star. She is not as radiant as she was, and not as cheerful, but she is more centered; she has more gravity. She says she is happier and more secure. She dismisses the woman I fell in love with—herself at twenty-one years old—as having been still a child. She did not like herself as a child.

When she was thirteen, while her father was working for the United States Information Agency in India, Maxie was sent to Woodstock, a boarding school in the foothills of the Himalayas. Packed in her trunk were ten boxes of Kotex that her mother had bought in New Delhi. Humiliated by her mother's anticipation, Maxie hid the boxes on the shelf of her closet and at the end of the term repacked them, unused and musty, for the trip back down to the plains, where she abandoned them under her bed when the family, a month later, left for the United States on home leave.

During the boat trip from Bombay to Naples, her family dined with an Anglo-Indian named Anthony Hart, who was on his way back to the University of Chicago, where he taught mathematics. He wore colorful American sport shirts, used American slang he learned from his students, and shortened his British vowels so he would sound more American.

"Isn't he handsome," Maxie said to her mother after their first lunch on shipboard. The question was not entirely rhetorical. Because she had just read a book called *The Facts of Life and Love for Teen-Agers*, in which the facts were arranged like a quiz in questions and answers, she assumed that love was a subject you could study and master, like history. Anthony was a question, and she wanted her mother to tell her if her attraction to him was the correct answer.

He had a narrow face, like that of an El Greco saint, and the kind of arched nose she would forever after look for in her lovers—and which she claims I have. That evening, for the first dinner at sea, he ordered wine for four. Maxie straightened her shoulders and fingered the stem of the wine glass that was put in front of her. She tried not to look at her mother or father. Aware of how delighted she was to be included among the adults, Anthony asked her—adult to adult—what she thought of the wine. Mimicking a movie she had once seen, she said, "It's adequate."

Her father laughed, her mother smiled; and Maxie felt a blush prickling her cheeks and forehead. Under the table, she pinched her thigh to block her tears with pain.

Anthony, seeing Maxie redden, sipped from his glass and agreed, "It's adequate."

She knew he was being kind; but, although she was embarrassed by his concern, she was grateful for it. After the costume dance that followed supper, she found him smoking a cigarette alone in the glassed-in observation deck. The bulbs set in the ceiling cast small pools of light like greatly enlarged perforations along the floor. The seas were rough, and every time she heard a louder-than-usual creaking she thought the ship was about to rip in half. She imagined Anthony saving her; she imagined them huddling in a life boat, the surrounding world dark except for a glow beneath the water where the ship, still blazing with party lights, was slowly sinking.

She stood beside him, propping her elbows—as he had—on the railing that ran below the windows. She wanted to thank him for having been kind to her during supper without having to admit that she was ashamed of what she had said about the wine. The room smelled of salt air and floor wax. The lights above them turned the long glass panels into an indistinct mirror. If she looked closely she could see an inflamed pimple on the wing of her left nostril, which she tried to hide, when she turned to him, by pretending to scratch her cheek.

"At supper—" she began.

"Should we have sent the wine back?" He boosted them both over the embarrassing moment by interrupting her. "Wasn't it terrible junk?"

"My father laughed at me," she said.

"He just didn't realize how grown up you were," he said.

"When I act grown up," she said, "people laugh at me."

"I didn't laugh at you," he said.

They had both turned so their backs were against the railing. Maxie squeezed her eyes shut, opened them, took a deep breath, and said, "Will you kiss me?"

"I think you drank too much," said Anthony.

"Please, kiss me," she said.

"Maxie," he said, "you know I can't."

"You don't want to?" she asked.

"I'm twenty years older than you," he said.

Tiptoeing up, she threw her arms around him. He reached behind his neck and unlocked her hands as easily as he'd unsnap a necklace she'd fastened around his throat as a joke.

"I'd better go," he said; and, having squeezed her hands fraternally, he left the room.

Maxie, dressed in the red gauzy Indian dancing-girl outfit that she had worn to the costume party, shivered in the dim light and stamped her feet so she could listen to the jingling of the bells that were strapped around her ankles.

Later in her parents' stateroom, she sat cross-legged in her blue pajamas at the foot of the lower bunk while her mother sorted through the clothes in a suitcase.

"When will men want to kiss me?" she asked.

"Don't your boyfriends want to kiss you?" her mother asked back.

"I don't have any boyfriends," Maxie said.

"You're still thirteen," her mother said.

"Sigrid's thirteen," Maxie said. "Boys want to kiss her."

Sigrid was her roommate at Woodstock. She always left her opened box of Kotex under the sink in their room and warned Maxie not to use any. Maxie, pretending to be disgusted at the idea, would say, "Gross. I don't need them." And, as soon as she had a chance, she would check to see if there were any signs that Sigrid had found the unopened supply, hidden in Maxie's closet.

While Maxie shopped with her mother on the stopover in Naples, they were surrounded by urchins who jabbered at them in Italian. When Maxie lagged to glance at a scarf in a store window, one of the boys asked in accented English, "You wanna fuck?" She tried to ignore him and hurried, wobbling on her high heels, to catch up with her mother; but the kid chased after her, shouting, "You wanna fuck? You wanna fuck?" Her face burning, trying not to cry, she fell into step beside her mother, matching the longer stride by nearly loping along the pavement, feeling protected within the adult rhythm of her mother's walk.

They left Naples on the *Leonardo da Vinci*. It was February. Disturbed by the rough seas, Maxie woke and stumbled through the stateroom to the bathroom to urinate. When she wiped herself, blood soaked through the tissue. She roused her mother, who fished in her suitcase for a box of Italian sanitary napkins she had bought in the ship's boutique. As her mother handed one to her, she said, "These will be the fanciest napkins you'll ever use." Maxie held by its string the dainty net bag in which the napkin was packaged, as though it were one of the bags of gold-foil-wrapped chocolates she used to receive as a child on Easter; and she wondered, not at how her body could become alien, but at how suddenly the alien could become familiar.

Maxie had chattered this story out, nervously, her after-sex energy making her shiver in my arms, that night before I left for New York, the night I had come inside her when we had used no contraception. We had finished making love, and I was drifting into sleep (the image: a ship, sails billowing red in a setting sun, growing smaller and smaller until the speck on the horizon changed from a ship into sleep itself, a terrible engine that roared straight at me, obliterating me). Maxie was curled, facing me, her knees raised fetally, one leg thrown over my body.

Suddenly, she had stiffened, flipped onto her back, said, "Dennis, I can't sleep," and started reciting her memories, carefully and in detail, as though they formed a story that she often had told herself. She kept interrupting herself to say "This is very important" or "Are you paying attention?"

When I asked her, "Why is this important?" she struggled in the coil of bed sheets for a moment and then plunged free of the covers, staggering across the bedroom floor. The breeze from the open window pressed like a hand against her nightgown. She left the bedroom and, after a while, returned carrying a glass of water high as though it were a lit candle, illuminating her way.

"Look . . ." she said, plumping into bed after gulping the water; but what she meant was: listen.

During home leave, her family stayed with her grandparents in Pelham, a northern suburb of New York City. A few days before they arrived, someone had broken into the house through a cellar window and, frustrated by the bolted kitchen door at the top of the cellar stairs, had stolen from the laundry room a dirty pillow case, a pair of pajama bottoms, a man's white dress shirt, and one of Maxie's grandmother's voluminous bras.

While baby-sitting for her younger brothers the first weekend of their stay, Maxie answered the telephone and told the man on the other end of the line who asked to speak with her parents that her parents were not at home, that nobody was at home except her and her brothers, could he call back?

"How many brothers do you have?" the man asked.

"Four," said Maxie.

"How old are they?" he asked.

"Two, five, seven, and nine," she said.

"How old are you?" he asked.

"Thirteen, almost fourteen," she said.

"You're a big girl," he said. "What kind of underpants do you wear?"

Maxie hung up the phone. He called back. She hung up to disconnect the call and then took the receiver off the hook. The rest of the night she spent squatting in the room where her brothers slept, peering through the curtained windows at the sidewalk in front of the house, convinced the caller was the housebreaker, who would soon drive up, hunting for her.

A few days later, Maxie's mother called her into the bedroom. Lying across the spread on tissue paper was a tiny white Maidenform bra. Maxie, so embarrassed by every sign she was becoming a woman that she pretended not to understand any reference to sex that skimmed through her parents' conversation, mumbled, "Thanks," grabbed the bra by the strap as though she were picking up one of her brother's damp diapers, and ran to the room she was using on the third floor. In India, bras were difficult to find; and the coarse Indian underwear was, among the girls at Woodstock, notoriously unacceptable.

Alone, she stripped off her blouse and tried on the

bra. She knew that the size, 28 AAA, was laughably small. Real bra sizes were in the 30's, and cup sizes were at least A, preferably B or C. So this meager cotton contraption would be as scorned as admired back at school. Still it was a promise; and, during the boat trip from New York to Naples, she conspired with another thirteen-year-old girl she had met on the ship—Lenore McCurry—to find out what it would feel like to nurse a baby. Hidden in a bathroom, they lifted their sweaters. Lenore's nipples were small wrinkled bumps ringed by narrow brown bands that reminded Maxie of *puris*, puffs of crisp Indian bread; and she couldn't find the hole through which she knew milk was supposed to come. When she sucked, the nipple felt like a ball of chewed gum between her lips.

"What does it feel like?" she asked Lenore.

"Tickles and sort of hurts," Lenore said. "What does it feel like to do it?"

"I don't know," said Maxie, not sure of how to describe it. "You do it to me now."

When Lenore did, Maxie felt a puzzling sympathetic tingling in her other breast.

"A boyfriend of mine wanted to do it," Lenore said.

"Did you let him?" asked Maxie.

"He said he loved me, and I should let him," Lenore said, "but I didn't."

"If a boy loved me," Maxie said, "I'd let him."

"What if you had a baby?" Lenore asked.

"How would I get a baby letting him do that?" Maxie asked.

Unable to explain the connection she knew existed, Lenore said, "I'd never let him."

On a side trip to Rome, Maxie's mother took the five children to St. Peter's on a ceremonial day, when the Pope was to appear. The crowd was thick, and Maxie got separated from her family in the press of bodies. While straining to catch a glimpse of the Pope, she realized that the man in front of her was pressing his left hand into the crotch of her dress, rubbing his fingers against the bony protrusion where her pubic hair was beginning to sprout. She backed away and, squirming through the crowd, found Amanda, her brothers' *ayah*, whom she tried unsuccessfully to ask about what had just happened. But, ashamed by both the event and her naiveté, she could not frame the question clearly; and Amanda, misunderstanding her, thought she was asking why there was such a great crowd.

"Because it's a holiday," she told Maxie, who for the rest of the trip back to India would wrestle alone with the mystery of lust.

When she was nine, her mother had explained the facts of life. Men put their penises into women to make babies. The sperm came out of the penis and swam up inside the woman to meet the egg. Maxie accepted this description and, after discussing it with a friend, named the process *egging*. Judging from the frequency of the arrival of a new baby in her family, she figured that married couples went through this egging ordeal once or twice a year, allowing for a few failures in fertilization. On the trip from New York to Naples, when she discovered, in a *Reader's Digest* that someone had left near her deck chair, that married couples on the average had intercourse two or three times a week, she was shocked—although she was beginning to understand that there was some kind of pleasure a man got from his penis in conjunction with a feminine presence. She also knew that a woman got some gratification from "love," which meant catching a man, being devoted to him, and, as a reward for letting you be so attached to him, letting him put his penis inside you somehow.

What she failed to understand was why the man in St. Peter's had stuck his hand in her crotch. What kind of pleasure could he get by rubbing her down there with his fingers? The only possibility she could puzzle out was that a man got some perverse satisfaction out of humiliating a female by touching her in a private place. She was ashamed. But what had she done to deserve being treated like that? The only thing that had provoked such demeaning treatment was the fact that she was a girl. Therefore, she concluded, it was just being a girl that she was ashamed of.

"Do you understand?" she asked, brushing her fingers across my crotch as though to both check for and invite an inappropriate aroused response—and picturing her downy teenaged pudenda and her unformed breasts did excite me—which she got.

"Oh, Dennis . . ." she said, disappointed. And pleased.

That night in Rome, she asked her mother, "If a man wants to touch you, does that mean he loves you?"

"A man who loves you will want to touch you," her mother carefully answered, "but there are lots of men who will want to touch you who won't love you."

"How can you tell the difference?" Maxie asked.

"When you grow up," her mother said, "you'll know."

Thinking of the man in the crowd and thinking that she was growing up too slowly for what was happening to her, she wailed, "How long will it take?"

Her second period was late; and, back at Woodstock, she lived in fear that it would arrive without her knowledge or would catch her unprepared, staining the back of her skirt. She developed terrible itches on her labia that required vigorous scratching. She would rub, feeling a sensation that was both pleasurable and painful, the way a sunburn sometimes feels under a needle-point shower, until the surface capillaries ruptured and little dots of blood began to stain her underpants, stains she hoped were signs that her second period had begun.

When her second period finally started, her roommate, Sigrid, gave her one of her Junior Tampaxes.

"How can you use those horrible things?" Sigrid asked, pointing at the bulky rectangular Indian Kotex that Maxie held.

Maxie went into the bathroom and poked her finger inside herself to see what the space was like. It seemed like a very narrow passageway for something as large as a Tampax, let alone a baby. She slipped the tip of the Tampax in, trying to imagine what it would be like to have a man shove his penis up. She was beginning to get the idea that women were supposed to get some kind of pleasure when men entered them. But the Tampax didn't give her any kick, so, after wadding the barely used cotton tube in fists of toilet paper and hiding it at the bottom of the wastebasket, she snapped a Kotex into place, adjusted the belt, and, emerging from the bathroom, lied to Sigrid about having used the Tampax.

During the term, she waited apprehensively, hopefully, for one of the boys at school to try to make love to her; but when vacation came, she returned unkissed, unfumbled, to New Delhi.

Her first night home, her mother found her curled on the bed, a sheet drawn over her head.

"I'm not pretty," she said, when her mother asked her what was wrong. "I want to be like Sigrid. All the boys want to dance with her."

She had once seen Sigrid being pressed against a wall in an empty classroom by a boy from the tenth grade. Her eyes had been closed. And, as the boy rubbed against her, she had slowly brought her hands up and gently touched his back. Maxie knew, if she had been in Sigrid's place, she would not have thought of touching the boy's back; and knowing that made her feel she would never be able to make anyone love her.

"I want to be pretty," she told her mother.

For four years, Maxie had been studying Bharatnatyam dancing; and Maxie's mother thought that, to cheer up her daughter, she would arrange a dance recital for charity in an Old Delhi theater she knew they could use.

"You'll be a star," she told Maxie.

"She'll get a lot of attention," she told her husband, "and maybe she won't feel like such an ugly duckling."

Maxie rehearsed for a month with her guru at Triveni Kala Sangum in downtown Delhi, where classical

Indian dancing and tabla playing were taught. She would stand, barefoot on the smooth cement floor, dressed in a Punjabi suit, stamping out her dance, as the teacher, an old man with close-cropped gray hair, tapped his finger cymbals together and sang *ta tiki ta ta, ta tiki ta.*

During the performance, the lights around the proscenium blinded her. The audience she could not see sounded like a wind rustling dry branches. She finished the dance, convinced that their restlessness proved they did not like her. After the show, she left her parents, who were backstage chatting with friends. Still dressed in her costume, made up, jasmine sprigs in her hair, she slipped from the stage door and headed across the dusty parking lot.

Halfway to her parents' blue station wagon, she was surrounded by fans, dozens of Indian men in dhotis, sticking their hands out to touch her. Terrified, trying not to run, she made it to the car, cracked open the door, and slid in. She closed and locked the door, rolled up the windows, and waited for her mother and father to rescue her.

The men surrounded the car and peered at her. They reached out longingly and cried in English, "Pretty, pretty." Then, one by one, they bent down until they were all crouched around the car, their wet lips flattened against the glass, kissing her through the windows.

As Maxie talked, it was as though she were dilating, opening up to me, allowing me to peer into her soul. What I saw was not familiar. If Maxie had become a stranger to her mother after marrying me, she—at least temporarily—seemed a stranger to me after telling me this story. She had become as alien as everything else in my life had become.

"Why did you tell me all this now?" I asked.

She flopped over, facing away from me.

"I'm tired," she said.

For a long while, I watched her, her shoulders slowly rising and falling with her breathing, the way she startled once or twice—she must have been having a falling dream—the way she rubbed her side with her elbow. Not only did her story make her seem strange; she even looked unfamiliar. It was as though, in the nine years we had been together, I never had noticed she had aged until now.

When I met Maxie, the summer before my senior year at Amherst College and her senior year at Smith, she looked like Mary who cowers against the wall in Rosetti's *Ecce Ancilla Domini,* a picture I had studied in art appreciation class the year before. She would make lunches, which we ate on the mountain behind the Valley Players, the stock theater in Holyoke where we both were apprenticing. Above us on the hillside, bulldozers chugged away at building the next winter's ski slopes. We lay back on the grass, listening to the jets from Westover Field roaring their nuclear payloads back and forth like confused geese. She listened to my amorous imploring and said no. She kept her ankles crossed and her thighs squeezed together.

One rainy night, while the audience of thirty huddled in the front row of the six-hundred-seat theater, I tumbled Maxie on the musty curtains in the subbasement storage room. While we were tangled, a short circuit set a kerosene-soaked rag on fire; the rag set the paint room on fire; the paint room set the back of the theater on fire.

Hearing more muffled thumps than there should have been in the second act, I pulled on my pants. Struggling into my jersey, I ran up the stairs to investigate. I have always been an alarmist, but usually I am disappointed.

Not that night. The paint room was at the top of the second flight of stairs. I turned on the landing and faced a crackling, exploding wall of flames. The colors were beautiful: crimson, orange, yellow, blue. Charging down the steps, I slammed into the curtain room.

Maxie sat, naked, in the rumpled cloth. I glanced for her clothes, grabbed them, and held them out to her.

She shook her head.

"Get dressed, Maxie," I said. "The whole theater's on fire."

She shook her head.

Smoke curled down the stairs, along the floor, into the room. There were no windows or exits in the sub-basement. I poked the clothes at her face.

"Maxie!" I screamed.

She shook me away. I hopped from one leg to the other. She heaved a deep sigh and, blinking back tears, explained:

"I'm not a virgin anymore."

She folded her hands and bowed her head. Softly, so softly that I could barely hear her over the booming fire upstairs, she asked me to leave her alone.

"Maxie," I said, tapping her shoulder.

She looked up and asked:

"What?"

"You're crazy," I said.

I punched her in the jaw as hard as I could, slung her over my shoulder, and carried her out of the room.

Stumbling blindly through the smoke, I climbed the first flight. Flames licked down the stairs from above. I edged by them toward the lumber-loading door, which I kicked open. The fire cast dancing red spooks on the woods behind the theater. I jumped off the platform. Fire engines whined to the left. Instead of going along the driveway, I climbed the slope to the right. By the time I had plumped Maxie onto the grass, we were both drenched.

She stirred. I sat beside her. Under the assault of rain and firehose, the theater hissed. A single red tongue flickered from the door I had left open. Just like a huge lizard.

My vision of catastrophe went up in smoke. I grimaced in embarrassment at having beaten—I waited for the magenta swelling to disfigure her jaw—and bodily carried my naked love to a fairly public hill, saving her from only watering eyes and a smoky cough or two. After I helped her into my shirt, we crept to my car. While she huddled in the back seat, I retrieved her clothes from the damaged building.

Maxie and I—and the other apprentices—rebuilt flats while carpenters rebuilt the three gutted rooms and while electricians rewired the otherwise unharmed theater. Pirandello waited in the wings for a week. We examined trunks of costumes for damage, sauntering away with Godotesque derbies and crystal-knobbed canes.

There followed a lyrical interlude. We pranced in costumes. We made love in the fields. We were demure townsfolk in *The Teahouse of the August Moon*. At four Sunday morning, after striking the set, we curled up on the curtains in the storeroom.

Toward the summer's end, Maxie sang solo in *The Boy Friend*. Maxie's mother arrived on Thursday to see the show. Mrs. Witheral was a small handsome woman with close-cropped hair and features that were saved from being severe by a sad, comical droop to her mouth. She met us for dinner, dressed entirely in green. Even the angular frames of her glasses were green.

We sat in a seafood restaurant beside a wall cluttered with the photographic history of the restaurateur, a tired-looking fat man who from the evidence must have spent a major part of his years shaking hands with minor starlets and being initiated into King Neptune's Club on ships that forever were crossing the Equator. Mrs. Witheral kept peering at me over the top of her raised menu.

Between the cherrystone clams and the swordfish, she advised us both to keep our heads, to take precautions, and to distrust adolescent infatuation.

Maxie leaned across the table.

"We're not adolescents, Mother," she said.

Mrs. Witheral raised her eyebrows.

"Then," she said, "you're old enough not to trust love too easily or too much."

We murmured polite incoherent phrases inaudibly. The last show of the summer was *The Desperate Hours*, a play about a family held hostage in their home by criminals. On stage, the crew built a two-story house with six rooms, two staircases, and no fourth wall. Maxie and I, in our free time, when no one else was in the theater, would dress as Elizabethans or as members of the Sun Court and play hide-and-seek in the complicated set. We crept up stairways, listening for telltale floor-creaks; flattened ourselves against walls; slipped through partially opened doors. The house was a labyrinth; and we, playing first one role and then the other, were Theseus or the beast. Or, if another apprentice skipped supper to join our game, Maxie and I were transformed from Greeks to Germans; and our golden thread metamorphosed into bread crumbs as we Hansel-and-Greteled our way through the Black Forest, trying to avoid the witch.

To be discreet, we slept in the theater. No men were allowed in Maxie's apartment house; and whenever I climbed the steps to my room, my landlady cracked open her door to spy. At night, when Maxie would brood and I would insist on knowing what troubled her, she would cock her head to the side, pull back her hands with a touch-me-not gesture, and plucking with all her fingers as though trying a sticky surface, say what became her refrain, "You can't have everything." Then she would give me a wonderfully bland smile.

Her moodiness increased. Frustrated and impatient with her, I began losing my temper. During a performance, as we waited backstage for the final curtain, she lifted the hand that I had absent-mindedly and affectionately placed on her shoulder, and curled from under my arm. I was astounded. I hunched angrily forward to demand an explanation. The curtain rushed down. Applause exploded. I was carried onto the set by the press of bodies and habit.

After the show, I sat on the end of a wagon in the shop, waiting for the theater to empty. The stage manager wandered about the set, picking up third-act props and replacing them with first-act props. One by one, the actors, with pink rims along their hairlines and flushes of color under their chins, patting their sweaty necks or trying to dig grease paint out of their ears, walked across the stage and through the door into the parking lot. The stage manager rang up the curtain for the night, yawned, called good-bye, and followed them.

Maxie hesitated in the wings, then made her entrance. When I reached for her hands, she pulled away. In the past, clutching her hands to her breast had been a coy invitation. Now she was merely withdrawing. But the gesture was the same, and the similarity jarred, as though her recoiling hands were third-act props the stage manager had forgotten to remove from the first-act set.

The familiarity of the move betrayed her intent. Instead of putting me off, it triggered love, a reflex conditioned by our summer romp. I reached for her again, knowing as I did that she would reject me, knowing that if she rejected me I would get angry—not because of the rejection, but because of her stupidity. She was trying to tell me something important; and, by changing the meaning of the gesture, she was making it impossible for me to understand. It was as though she were gabbling her warning in a foreign language.

She shrugged me away, and I grabbed her wrist. She tried to pry loose my fingers. We struggled silently. When she found she couldn't free herself, she said, "I think I want to go home tonight. Will you drive me?"

By phrasing it so casually—"I *think* I want to go home . . ."—she was denying that anything was changing between us. If she refused to admit that now, it would make it harder for us to talk about it, to deal with it later. Driving her home—I thought—would seal our separation.

"I want to talk to you," I said.

"Then let me go," she said.

"Will you promise to stay and talk?" I asked.

She nodded yes.

I released her wrist. We stood for a moment face to face, and then she bolted upstage. She yanked on a fake door, and the set trembled. I grabbed her by the shoulders.

"You said you'd let me go," she said.

"You promised not to run away," I said.

Rapidly blinking to keep from weeping, she said, "It's so unfair. You're stronger than me. I don't want to talk to you."

She was right. It was unfair. I wanted to let her go, but I didn't want my strength to be a weakness. Had we been evenly matched, perhaps I still could have held her. Her complaint was a strategy. After all, there are no fair fights. You win however you can.

Abruptly, free of any concern for her, all I wanted to do was win. I felt a shifting of psychic masses as though my brain were a planet with sliding continents. Up until this moment, I had lived my life the way I had wrestled on my high school team. I didn't care enough about the game to drive to the end; winning was always a gift. If in my life I had succeeded more often than I had failed, it was because I had been lucky enough to grow up with parents who had been willing to or needed to grant me the present of unearned victories. Maxie was not so inclined.

Her wanting to win made me want to win. Our old bond, having failed, had created a new bond. We were joined through the force we exercised against each other. It was as though we were on opposite lips of a chasm. Reaching across the gulf to touch hands had made us fall. Now, only by pushing against each other did we keep from plummeting into the pit.

With a satisfying access to cruelty, the comfortable engaging of complementary gears, I twisted Maxie's arm and asked, "What's the matter?"

She spoke oracularly out of an alien mouth, smaller and tighter than I had known:

"I'm pregnant."

The abortion punctuated the end of summer, not, I think, with an exclamation point, but with a question mark. Maxie and I warily circled each other's affection, not sure of what to do with a new tenderness, which followed a surprising guilt. We were not ashamed of having had the abortion, but we were ashamed of having failed a test that we had not been aware we were taking until it was over. As with *koans*, the impossible Zen riddles we used to ask each other, there were no correct answers. Having the baby was not the point. For the first time in my life, my own youth caught me by surprise. It was as though, by entering into a relationship with Maxie, I had posed myself a question that the progress of our relationship would answer.

"Why did you go back inside me?" Maxie asked that night in Springfield after she had finished telling me her story.

"I suddenly became afraid," I said.

"Of not having children?" she asked.

"Of not wanting them," I said.

In the dark, I slipped off Carla's couch and, after fumbling about for my clothes, felt my way to the bathroom. I closed the door and, after walking back and forth through the tiny room a dozen times, caught hold of and pulled the light cord.

My face, squinting eyes and puffy cheeks, was someone else's face. My chin was smeared with blood from the cut in Carla's thumb, which must have started bleeding again while we were bouncing on her couch. I rinsed off the blood. I dragged a blue towel from a rack and wiped the sticky thread that, like a cobweb, connected my thigh to my genitals. I dressed.

I felt emptied as though someone had split me down the front and, pressing huge thumbs on my back, had cracked open my rib cage and turned me inside out. When I walked into the living room, I saw, in the light from the bathroom, Carla's open eyes suddenly close. She was pretending to be asleep; so, pretending I believed her, I left.

"Don't turn on the light," said my grandfather.

He was sitting in the desk chair at the foot of the bed, a motionless silhouette in the semidark hotel room. My father, asleep, sprawled diagonally across the mattress, his bare left leg sticking out from under the crumpled sheet. His clothes, neatly folded, lay on the bureau. A neon sign across the street from the hotel lit the room with an uncanny orange-brown glow, making the still scene look like an old sepia photograph.

"We came back here about eleven," he said. "What time is it now?"

"Two," I said.

"I've been sitting here all that time," he said. "No wonder I'm stiff. Moses got very drunk."

I sank into the easy chair in the corner of the room across from my grandfather. Between us, on the bed, my father smacked his lips, joining in our conversation with sleep-talk.

"I thought I'd better stay here with him until you got back," said my grandfather. "He always thought I didn't take care of him."

"Do you like him?" I asked.

"He's my son," he said.

"A father doesn't have to like his son," I said.

"He's proud of what you're doing," said my grandfather.

"Proud of the farm?" I asked.

"Not just the farm," he said. "But you left your job when you stopped enjoying it. You moved to the country. You do what you want to do."

"I don't know what I want to do," I protested.

"He thinks you do," said my grandfather. "He thinks you've escaped the traps he fell into. He thinks you're not going to make the same mistakes he made. He told me that's one of the reasons he left home."

"He was imitating me?" I asked. I had been afraid of being a model for a child; I never thought I would be a model for a parent. "What does he think I'm doing?"

"I felt the same thing about him when he got his first teaching job," he said. "That he wasn't going to make the same mistakes I made. He didn't. He made his own mistakes."

"How do you know?" I angrily asked. My grandfather had been separated from my father for so many years, he couldn't know him. He had no right to judge him.

"I can tell," he said.

"How?" I asked. "From seeing him once every ten or fifteen years? From my mother's letters? From seeing what he's like tonight?"

"He couldn't be that different tonight from the way he usually is," said my grandfather. "Even though he's run away, he couldn't be that different. Is he?"

I could not answer. He seemed different. But it also seemed that I was just seeing him differently.

I did not want to fight with my grandfather, and I was not even sure that I had a right to accuse him of not understanding my father. I had spent more time with my father than he had, but I didn't understand him. Maybe time did not matter.

"What were his mistakes?" I asked.

"He never stops teaching," he said.

"You mean he's too generous," I said.

"You're very much like him," he said. "You shouldn't hate him for making mistakes. Just because he ran away from home doesn't mean he doesn't love his family."

After a long silent interval, perhaps five minutes, my grandfather stood and, picking up his coat from the chair back, crossed the room. Before leaving, he said:

"Make sure Moses knows I stayed with him until you arrived."

When my father woke an hour after my grandfather left, he immediately asked:

"Where's my father?"

"He carried you up here," I said, "and stayed with you until I came."

My father sat on the edge of the bed, his boxer shorts bagging around his surprisingly thin thighs. He bent over, rubbing his face with his palms, and said, "He's gone?"

"He told me to make sure you knew he waited," I said.

My father nodded and then said, "Let's go home."

We rented a car. I had expected my father to spend the drive north to Massachusetts talking over the past few days, trying in his teacher's way, by altering the words used to describe the events, to alter the events themselves. Instead, he was uncharacteristically silent, answering my questions with a word or two when he answered at all.

We reached Springfield at dawn. I parked in front of my parents' house at the top of the hill. We both climbed out, stretched, and stood together on the sidewalk. After turning up his jacket collar against the chill, he said, "When I was at your farm you told me you thought fathers have to choose between destroying their children or being destroyed by them. Do you remember?"

I nodded.

"Do you really believe that?" he asked.

"I did," I said.

"Do you now?" he asked.

"I don't want to believe it," I said.

My father gave me a look—of impatience or disgust, I could not tell which.

"That night at the farm—we never decided," he said. "Do you think I destroyed you?"

"No," I said.

"Do you think I tried to?" he asked.

"No," I said.

"Do you think I wanted to?" he asked.

"No," I said.

His directness made me uncomfortable—not because it was direct, but because it seemed a pose, as though he really was not being direct at all, and his open, forceful manner hid some premeditated program. We were not having a conversation; my father was drawing me into a Socratic dialogue. He was trying to teach me something.

Wanting to learn, I asked, "Do you think I've tried to destroy you?"

"Do you?" he asked back.

He was the teacher; I was the pupil.

We were standing about a foot apart, face to face, as we had by the stream behind the farm where we had almost fought. And I felt the same tension between us, except instead of anger now it was love.

I grabbed my father's arm and squeezed it hard. He winced and with a yank pulled me close in a hug. We stood for a moment, embracing, then started edging away from each other, he toward the house, I toward the car.

"Tell Maxie I'm sorry about what happened," he said.

"I will," I said.

My father stopped moving toward the house. I stopped moving toward the car.

"You slept with Carla?" he asked.

I nodded.

He gestured down the hill.

"Think you can beat me to the end of the block?" he asked.

"Sure," I said.

"Ready," he said, "go."

The wind stinging my eyes, I ran down the slope to the corner of Maplewood Terrace and Ft. Pleasant Avenue. Gasping, tasting something antiseptic and bitter under my tongue, my head throbbing, I turned. My father stood at the top of the hill. He stooped to pick up a torn newspaper and climbed the steps to his home.